C

Even Trevi

WILL CRUMBLE

MW01250460

One Day
Even Trevi
WILL CRUMBLE

Neale McDevitt

TORONTO

Exile Editions
2002

This edition is published by Exile Editions Limited,
20 Dale Avenue, Toronto, Ontario, Canada   M4W 1K4

Sales Distribution:
McArthur & Company
c/o Harper Collins
1995 Markham Road
Toronto, ON
M1B 5M8
toll free:
1 800 387 0117
(fax) 1 800 668 5788

Design & Composition by TIM HANNA
Cover Design by ZERO WEATHER
Cover Painting by ROB ELLIOTT
Typeset at MOONS OF JUPITER
Final Formatting by MICHAEL CALLAGHAN
Author Photograph by EDWARD BAGARES
Printed and Bound at TRANSCONTINENTAL PRINTING

The publisher wishes to acknowledge
the assistance toward publication of
the Canada Council and the Ontario Arts Council.

ISBN 1-55096-554-9
Printed in Canada

This book is dedicated to my family and friends,
the people who have given me my stories
and language and love.

CONTENTS

THE McVIE CHRONICLES

OTHER STORIES

The McVie Chronicles

Notre-Dame-de-Grâce

I've spent my entire life in the same neighbourhood of Montreal. Officially it's called Notre-Dame-de-Grâce, French for Our Lady of Grace, but most people refer to it as NDG. Some kids snicker that NDG stands for Naked Dancing Girls. Others say it's for No Damn Good. All I know is that there is precious little grace to be found in these streets. Maybe I'm being a little harsh. In general, NDG is a nice place, with lots of kids and dogs trotting up and down its grid of tree-lined streets. But, it also has its share of hard patches; places where kids are warned not to wander, and corners that seem to collect the wild ones like greasy water pools in a pothole. Cops patrol these rough stretches in slow rolling cars, surveying the concrete scene with eyes plucked from Belfast soldiers.

I live in a hard patch, right along Sherbrooke Street, one of Montreal's busiest thoroughfares. Our stretch of Sherbrooke has been falling to shit for years, with closed-down businesses being replaced more and more by pawnshops and tattoo parlours. I guess it isn't all bad, though. For one thing, we've got green spots. There's Needle Park, where the local junkies go to commune with nature, and tiny triangular Skinhead Park, where the white supremacists of tomorrow gather for a little beer and a healthy exchange of ideas.

Like all inner city neighbourhoods, NDG has its collection of lunatics and bums. There are the low-level loons; transient shadows with smelly beards and mountain climber tans who shuffle in and out of the frame too quickly for us to take notice of their particular brand of dementia. Just another wild man hurtling down the street in oversized galoshes yelling holes through the clouds. One second he's squaring off against the cosmos, the next — poof! — he's gone. Cosmos: 9,198,786, 853 — Lunatics: 0.

Then we have the eccentrics who plop down in the booth at Dunkin' Donuts with a thud and a sigh while extracting an armful of sacred papers from under their jackets. Often they are students, those brilliant but off-kilter boys and girls who seem to congregate in ivory towers like doomed Capistrano swallows. They burn strange, but bright.

By the time they hit their late twenties, however, the fire has run its course, consuming their dazzlingly disarrayed intellectual gifts and leaving nothing but smouldering and uninspired madness. No longer can they be found in the great libraries clutching volumes of Sartre and scribbling copious notes. Instead they roost in 24-hour doughnut shacks, poetry and philosophy having given way to minestrone soup and brioches as sustenance.

Then there are NDG's resident nutbars who've been around as long as any one of us. Real institutions of alternative thought. We have Agent Orange, a Brylcreemed gent who marches down the street like a Russian soldier in a May Day parade, stopping only to deliver slow-motion karate chops to unsuspecting trees. Next up there's Barry the Dog Boy whose mind-bending combination of Tourette's and multiple personality disorder has blessed him with the alarming ability to bark like fifteen species of dogs. And, batting third, there's The Mayor, who spends the bulk of his days leaning precariously from his fourth-floor balcony delivering diatribes about Horton hearing a Who and waving to pedestrians in a manner befitting Queen Elizabeth. NDG all but drips with delusion and delirium. It's like the Poconos for the Halfway House set.

There's one guy named Lowry. He's a bent little blackguard who always wears a green army jacket and wool socks pulled up high over his pant legs. I don't know how crazy he is, but, in my grandpa's parlance, he sure is a mean old trout. Always cursing and cussing and snapping at passersby. Nothing but a grizzled sour face who's just one rubber rent cheque away from eking out the rest of his lemon-sucking days in an old Maytag box.

You always know when Lowry is coming because of the way he bangs down the pavement, scowling and grunting and kicking at trash cans. And it's a dead cinch guarantee that he'll have a bad mood on. He mistrusts the whole lot of us, even the smiling old dolls who spoon him out good, free, hot grub down at the soup kitchen. "Don't gyp me, woman," he'll hiss. "Top it off. Top it off!"

He hates us. Who knows why? Maybe he's holding a barbed grudge in his gut for some nasty bit of karmic misfortune that sent his life spinning into the crapper a thousand years ago. Maybe his father butt-fucked a curse-wielding gypsy. And maybe he's just a minor league sociopath carrying around a melon full of chemical imbalance. Probably, he's just a grouchy old shitheel.

But Lowry's got this companion, a fuzzy mutt named Scruffy. All scraggly fur and butt wiggle. The funny thing is, unlike his owner Scruffy just adores the world. He's always swinging over to folks with his tail tracing clockwise loops in the air and his tongue lolling around like a giddy stroke victim.

Why is it that the surly fuckers never stalk the streets with badass dogs that foam through rusted steel muzzles? Maybe it's God having a giggle by teaming up these antisocial miserables with the city's friendliest fur balls.

"How's Scruffy doing?" I asked Lowry one day.

"Fuck off, McVie," he snarled.

I just laughed and bent over to tickle Scruffy's chin. "Scruff, how the hell did a gold-plated pooch like you get stuck with a tarnished old turd bucket like him?" I jerked my thumb in Lowry's direction.

Lowry leaned over and cupped his hand to his ear, as if the dog were whispering D-Day coordinates to him. "Scruffy says, 'Go fuck yourself, you limp-dicked lush.'" He said it in a growly dog voice for effect. Lowry sure was a ball-buster all right, but there was a dose of Larry Olivier in him.

I played hurt. "Scruffy! I can't believe you'd say that." I clutched my heart. "I'm shocked. Outraged — and the lady I was with the other night would probably take great exception to any suggestion of my being impotent."

More Scruffy voice. "You call that unwashed, cumbersome brute a lady? More like something that'd run a horn through you during an African safari."

Unwashed comment aside, Lowry made a valid point; Corrine was a bit on the heavy side. She was a thick-boned woman with an impossibly hefty arse and large, muscled thighs that rubbed her corduroy pants bald between the legs. She definitely put the "large" in "largesse."

"A gnu," said Scruffy.

"Pardon me?"

"She's a fucking gnu. One of those wildebeests. Big, round mud-covered ass kerplunking down the game trail. Kerplunk, kerplunk." Lowry laughed and kerplunked his skinny butt back and forth as a visual. Scruffy just wagged his tail.

I was beginning to take exception to Scruffy's tone. Fun is fun, but Corrine was an OK woman. She was a big, happy soul and an enthusiastic practitioner of the oral love arts. "In fact," continued Scruffy, "I thought I saw some of those little para-site-eating birds perched on that ass-shelf of hers." (During their downtime from bumming, Scruffy and Lowry watch a lot of Discovery Channel. No one can deny that their knowledge of the wild kingdom is impressive.)

"Fuck you, Scruffy. And you too, Lowry. At least I'm getting laid."

"Right — if you call rattling a herbivore getting laid." Herbivore? Scruffy had a pretty good vocabulary for a lousy street mutt living on spare macaroni and beer nuts.

All the while Lowry is laughing like a stupid fucker. Laughing at everything that little cur said. Laughing at me. Laughing at Big Corrine and her big love. Laughing at the world and all of us who make an effort to live in it. I'd had enough of this bullshit. I got up, cuffed Lowry in the head and started off in the direction of the bar.

I spun around and booted Scruffy up his happy little arse.

There's also this couple living a few streets away. The Scream-ers. Every month or so they can be spotted, sure as my morn-ing shit, hollering and breaking up right there on the street. It's always the same. He'll be storming out in front, spitting poison back at his woman like an angry viper. "Fine. You don't like it, bitch? I'm fucking out of here." Twenty yards back, Mrs. Screamer will be trying to keep up with light-footed jogging steps. She'll fluctuate between calling him a no-good fuck-stick and pleading with him to come back. I'd seen the show, curtain to curtain, maybe two dozen times, late at night, broad daylight and early in the morning. It's never a bad time for the Dysfunctional Duo to break up.

One day I hit the streets on yet another mid-winter coffee run to Dunkin' Donuts. Bang. There he is speed walking and yahooing his goodbyes over his shoulder. "Colour me gone, you whore. I don't need your shit anymore." I pause to let her pass. Life had chewed on him pretty good over the years, he's ugly and whipped, but she's surprisingly sweet on the eyes. I've always admired the way she tucks her ass into tight jeans — she's a good woman to have walking in front of you.

"My shit?" she hollers. "All I want is for you to stop being a drunk. Is that so bad?" She wriggles on by and I swing into rank a couple of paces behind her.

The fight must have peaked somewhere on the last block because I could tell that she was about to start begging for him to come back. I could never figure out that part. Maybe he had wads of secret cash or a long, well-versed pecker — but I just couldn't see her addiction. "Let him go, sweetheart," I think to myself. "Try *this* drunk out for size instead."

They pass in front of the doughnut shop where she pulls up and bleats for him to stop. But her obvious agony has sewn little wings on his heels. He trundles even faster than before. I guess we're all like that in some way; we fight and get ugly and when we see that we have the person we love on the ropes, we start turning the silver screws. My father had a friend, a legend of the bar circuit, who used to regale my brother and me with tales of his days as a brawler. "Don't forget, boys," he'd whistle through his pulverized nose. "The fight only starts when the other guy hits the ground — that's when you put the boots to him."

Mrs. Screamer hits the ground. On her knees in a pile of greasy slush. Now she's pleading with him. "I'll die, Micky. I'll die without you." Right there in front of the big window of the doughnut shop. And it's a full house. Lowry's looking out. Billy and his new girlfriend. Murph. A couple of old queens are staring and shaking their heads. A table full of gawking students. But Mickey just keeps jack-rabbiting down the road.

She pounds the ground with fragile balled fists — "No! No! No!" — splattering browned snow and crap all over the place. She's blocking the way, so I'm kind of loitering on the corner, embarrassed for her and for me and for every fool who's ever let desperate love cross the threshold. By now, buddy — old Micky — is a full block away. A tiny shiver casts off from the small of her back and rides a tsunami all the way up to her head. She's dead quiet but shaking real hard. Her head drops and, there on her knees, she makes me feel like a guillotine is about to come slicing through the clouds. But, mercifully or not, there is a stay of execution and after an eternal second or two Mrs. Screamer climbs to her feet and bolts after her man.

I go in and order a large fortifying coffee and a fancy cherry-glaze doughnut made especially for Valentine's Day.

As I'm tucking into my glazer, a girl sitting in the booth in front of me says, "Was that pathetic, or what? On her knees begging."

Pathetic? Maybe. But maybe it's just the neighbourhood talking. Most of the long-time people here are like me. Lifers. We haven't lived in too many other places. We don't have all those bright, new horizons to distract us from our cul-de-sac reality. NDG love isn't high art or idyllic devotion. It's visceral and sad and, in many ways, it's based purely on white-knuckled survival. It isn't ephemeral and it surely doesn't soar on gossamer wings. When we are shit-lucky enough to turn up love, or at least some unsuspecting soul who accepts us for being the sedentary, dreamless creatures we are, we hang on dangerously tight like the drowning man pulling down on his saviour.

No, it has nothing to do with self-conscious spirituality or the esoteric merging of souls. This warp of love is really just a primal need to band together, huddling against the red-eyed wolves of the night. It's a bodily dread that isn't marked by cloud-parting epiphanies and sudden clarity of vision. It's all about being up to your neck in black swamp water and feeling something big and scaly slide by your leg. Terror, but shared terror.

The wind whips up and bangs away at the doughnut shop's big, plate-glass window. *Rattle, rattle, rattle.* A madman at the door. The Screamers are out there somewhere in the grip of that big, scaly madman. I think of the two of them topping off the world with their horrible, inescapable, love and, strange as it may sound, I am envious.

My fellow patrons have stumbled into silence; the teenage girl shivers and leans into her boyfriend's new love; one of the fags discreetly locks little fingers with his partner; Lowry pats Scruffy curled up on his lap. Me? I pinch at a dirty quarter lurking low in my jacket pocket and try my damnedest to recollect the last two digits in Big Corrine's elusive telephone number. These are bad times for solitary thought.

The Lighthouse Keeper

The night before she left forever, her smarmy friends staged a dinner party and dubbed it The Last Supper. They had seen Grace come and go a dozen times before and they were annoyingly adept at the grand gesture. Some guy I didn't know hoisted his glass and toasted her sense of adventure. "I'm not sure how you two hooked up," he smirked over his black-framed hipster glasses. "Grace is a child of the world, McVie, and you've hardly stepped outside that claustrophobic little neighbourhood of yours."

Everyone laughed, except me. I took a mouthful of Italian red and let it sit until it bit at my gums. "I'm the fucking lighthouse, dickhead," I finally said long after people had started talking about other things. "I don't move and I don't change. The light on the rock." The whole pinch-faced crew stared at me like I was a frozen caveman all thawed out and stinking up their smoked salmon send-off. Everyone except her. Her small hand squeezed my knee under the table.

But Dickhead was right, Grace and I were as different as right and wrong. She was one of those rare flowers that busts up through our cities of ice and concrete spreading nothing but wild fragrance and colour. A real jar of honey, with a big belly laugh that rolled out of her small frame to bathe us all in a perfect happiness that wasn't even our own. Like God splashing warm summer rain on undeserving faces.

Me? I was just a low-rent grunt who ate from tin cans and followed sports in which men bled and broke each other's bodies. I was, as my granny liked to say, "a drinker" and, as such, I was yoked with many of the unsavoury qualities so often found in men of my disposition: I was unkempt, unpunctual and entirely unambitious.

I'd been in love with Grace for 22 years, starting the moment she first walked into Grade 11 English class wearing white painter pants and a checkered shirt. It was early fall, and as she walked toward her desk through the beams of sunlight, golden particles of chalk dust swirled halos in her wake. My boy's heart didn't stand a chance.

We sat beside each other that year, but we never dated or anything like that. I was too shit-scared to ask. She went to the Grad with some pretentious knob who anchored our *Reach for the Top* team and who eventually toodled off to Yale or Harvard. I got drunk on beer and teenage angst and missed the whole dance snoring on the floor of a buddy's basement. The next morning, I woke up fetalled around myself like a fiddlehead. A powerful mix of relief and sadness churned at the centre of my hangover — relief for not having gone to the dance and seeing her, sadness for the same. I'd shake the headache but the melancholy sank its claws in me for good.

Grace flitted in and out of my life for the next two decades. You know how hummingbirds look perfectly motionless even though they're whizzing at 1,000 wingbeats a second? That was Grace. Interested and in front of you one minute and — *whoosh* — gone in a slash of colour the next. She had happy feet and a curious mind. She really believed in the world and in all the lessons to be gleaned from its good and bad.

Personally, I didn't trust the fucking place, good or bad. Too many toothy creatures crouching in the reedy unknown. Instead, I grew fond of the familiar sounds and smells of my Montreal neighbourhood, NDG.

To me, nothing was as comforting as sitting down on my regular stool in my regular bar and having my regular beer — a cold Molson Ex — appear without having to ask. While Grace filled her years dancing through Europe, doing theatre in New York, and living on an ashram in India, I dug in and let my roots grow long and stubborn.

Sometimes we'd go years without seeing each other and then, suddenly, I'd get a homemade postcard from her. They never said where she was or what she was doing, usually just a line or two that twanged at my heart. "Thought I'd return some of my happiness back to its source," she wrote in one, signing it with a "G" and some hand-drawn palm trees.

Another time, we bumped into each other on the street and grabbed a bite to eat. She sat there laughing and shaking the snow from her close-cropped blond hair. She looked great, all lean and wide-eyed and sporting the greatest smile to ever split open a face. I sucked in my rolling gut and swallowed a rye-flavoured burp from the previous night. In a single instant I understood why I never ended up in the arms of graceful women like her. It was like being shot between the eyes with a diamond-tipped bullet of complete understanding.

But sometimes the gods give you a sip of the good stuff. Sometimes, after a month or so of ground beef and onions, they slide an expensive slip of Swiss chocolate into your mouth to momentarily cleanse your workaday palate. A beggar's tour of Heaven.

Just before last Christmas, Grace and I met at a bar where some band was launching an album. Grace knew the drummer and I was there because my buddy, the guy with the basement in high school, was the president of the record label — another one who had worked his way to success and happiness. Fucker. He always made sure I got invites to the events with free booze and finger food.

Grace looked beautiful as always, but I saw a dorsal fin of sadness circle in her eyes. Her fiancé had yanked the rug out from under her and she was nursing some big, bad wounds. I made it my mission to get her to laugh. I listed off a string of my monumental romantic failures: of moving in with a woman whom I met on the subway only to find that she was frightfully insane; of professing my love to another woman the exact moment she was to tell me that she finally realized she was gay; and of the drunken night I fell asleep between my lover's thighs while giving her head. Oh Grace laughed big and hard all right. I have a knack for making women do that.

We hung out in a corner and laughed all night. Laughed through the pomp, laughed through the circumstance. Laughed through her drummer friend's glare when we wouldn't shut up during the introductions. For the first time in my life, I was OK with who I was around her, OK being the only bowling shirt in a sea of designer clothes, OK with not having a cell phone or aspirations or a crushed velvet loft.

As the band rolled into its second set, Grace got serious. "It's all such a mystery, isn't it, McVie?" she asked.

"I spend most of my waking moments completely mystified," I replied honestly, absolutely no clue as to what she was talking about.

"Finding a partner and making things work. There's so much effort. Remember when we were kids, how simple it was?"

Swigging some beer, I shook my head. "Simple? I dunno. Love was always kind of rough on my boyhood self. It gave me the stutters and a goofy heart."

"Sure, but it was all just instinct, right? Your heart raced involuntarily. You couldn't help yourself. Love didn't have to be negotiated, it just happened."

I nodded, "Oh yeah. Love always just kind of kicked down my door and bitch-slapped me silly."

She smiled large but her eyes looked beaten. "I don't think I believe in true love anymore. Just the temporary, transient stuff."

I wanted to tell her to go right ahead and believe in big, true, full-time love, wanted to tell her that I'd loved her forever. Instead I just stared through my beer. She touched my hand and it gave me guts. "You know what I've always loved about me and you?" I asked. "I've never needed you to be mine — just knowing you were out there, somewhere, doing your thing, was good enough for me."

With that, she smiled a slice of magic into my eyes, took me by the hand and led me to the exit. In the background her drummer clanged a cymbal and shook his rock 'n' roll hair.

The next morning I lay on my back with my heavy arms looped up over my head. Her small breath warmed my shoulder and her hand pressed up against my heartbeat.

When I was a young giant, my heart tossed its thumps and bumps into the air with unthinking arrogance. That's OK, you know? OK to place your confidence in Chance when you're a cocky and resilient kid. It's a thrill to see where each beat might land. Sometimes they would float from the clouds like downy feathers off the swifts and swallows, landing lightly in the hair of perfumed ladies.

And sometimes my huge heartbeats were like darts from a blowgun. *Zip. Bingo!* Love in the afternoon. Sex later that night.

But in recent years, each beat lit up like a string of fireworks, jumping and arching high into the sky. The coloured explosions fanned ever outward and cast the women below in a distant lusty red. Yet each brilliant fireball would drop and drop and drop until it hissed goodbye in an anonymous lake below. It made me feel small and alone.

But there she was, asleep and freckled with heavenly blessings, catching each fading, loving, mighty, fragile beat in her hand. Just like that. She received my heart with absolute sleeping innocence and I was a giant again.

And so we happily rolled along for the next two weeks. I had never really bought into Christmas and that over-hyped injection of happiness we're supposed to mainline every year. But this time, wow. Days with her. Afternoons. Nights. Mornings together just laughing and writing and kissing and drinking cold tap water in her bed. We even snuck into our old high school and necked in the stairwell. Circle closed.

On Christmas Day I woke up before her. Aside from the lucky sheet twisted around one thigh, she was naked and exposed to all. The sun, ever her admirer, poured in through the slats of her old bamboo blinds, bathing her in delicate rays and tracing thin fingers along her glorious back and legs and shoulders and neck.

I propped myself up on an elbow and ran my undeserving eyes up and down her skin. She was so thin, so delicate, so vulnerable, so unlike the fleshy neighbourhood women I was usually drawn to. A sliver of grace and love and song and statuette carved by unseen hands. The centrepiece jewel in God's crown.

She stirred and I pressed my lips to her neck, my groin to her ass and everything else just fell into place. We lay there like two pieces of the most perfect jigsaw puzzle. At that moment I felt like we only needed one heart to keep us going.

"Who are you anyway, McVie?" she asked. "For you, I'm the strongest man in the world," I smiled. She chuckled and cupped my hand on her breast. And something about having her coiled safe in my arms and legs and feeling her tit beat in my hand made me feel like a strong man. Milos of Crete. Babe Ruth. John Wayne. A fucking Olympic champion.

"I'm helping you get ready," I whispered to the back of her head. She gave a half turn and my dick slipped from between the warmth of her ass cheeks. "Ready for what?"

"True and everlasting happiness," I said.

She started to laugh, but suddenly stopped. In that muted morning sun, her sun, she looked me square in my face and we both knew that what I said was true. The little flicker of sadness in her eyes told me that she also realized that her everlasting happiness wouldn't be with me.

But that was OK. I had known that all along.

See, all that loving was done in holiday time. Inflated time. All fat and succulent and slow moving — the perfect meal for the ravenous real world that was loping patiently along the game trail. It was just around the bend breathing hard and hungry.

"It's coming," I said to myself with resignation and a soft shudder as a distant howl tore through my sleep one night. Just hours before, she had told me she was leaving for L.A. soon into the New Year. I pressed up against her warm skin and gave in to bittersweet melancholy, trying to savour that last taste of divine chocolate as it melted away on my lips.

"They're calling for snow," Grace said, peeking up at the low-slung ceiling of cloud from the back of the cab that was taking us to the airport. I didn't look and I didn't say a word. Not even a grunt. Instead, I squeezed her deep into the crook of my arm. I felt like my granny trying to preserve spring forever by pressing flowers in the middle of fat dictionaries. But it was all in vain. Spring was nine inches deep in snow and Grace's eyes were far away, far away from me again.

At the airport I carried the bags and checked her in. We had one last beer in the lounge. Her blue eyes ran with the planes as they heaved themselves into the grey bellies of the clouds. I must've looked pitiful because when she saw me her beautiful face went sad. Sad and beautiful, the deadliest poison of all. Up came her hand, lovely bouquet of fingers, and anointed my lips. We'd hug and kiss later, but that was the last time we really touched.

And we whispered stuff. I remember every word, every devotion, every promise, every gratitude, every singsong of absolution and eternity, but I'm not telling now. Not telling ever, because love, like myth, needs its secrets to survive.

Then she was striding down the tunnel to the plane. I was stuck clay-footed at the gate with the other leave-behinds. Most were waving like fools or bawling "I love you." Me, I just stood there marvelling at her walk. Grace was excited, it showed in the double-time bob of her ass. Like the sooner she got her seat the sooner she'd be punching through new horizons. She wasn't happy to leave me, she was just happy to leave.

I watched her ankles and hamstrings. Watched her thin arms swing in their sockets. Watched the fine muscles in her back pull tight with each stride. Watched that neck on which I had gladly sacrificed 1,000 breathless kisses. Watched her spun-gold hair. Watched it all disappear.

Sweet shit, who's the cold bastard who drafted the rules for this game anyway? Into your life like a meteorite and then out again, just like that. Fuck Van Gogh and his petty gesture. Try having your heart carved out, you Dutch prick.

I was going to watch her plane take off from the big window, but it suddenly felt like a cornball thing to do. She never would have done it. Instead, I took a long, mournful piss and left.

Back home, I sparked the nub of a candle and put it in my window. Yeah, big bad lighthouse all right. I sat in bed for hours watching that small beacon burn low. Eventually it fizzled and died and I lay my head down in the dark. A plane droned overhead. People going somewhere. Away.

I shut my eyes and felt her skin on me again.

Same Shit, Different Millennium

January 1st, 2000. Happy goddamned New Year. The snow is gang-banging down the streets and the clouds are cruising low like fat-bellied, fully armed enemy battleships. Hell has iced up through and through and we're all encased in its lifeless grip. I'm warning you, people, it's a glacial La Brea Tar Pit out there, waiting to freeze us solid in our poses of apathy and desperation.

Lemme tell you university ass-scratchers something about global warming. It's all bullshit. Utter bullshit. Our ozone layer might be hot-rotting away from the inside and the polar ice caps might be hemorrhaging and doing a slow bleed back into the sea, but this fucking world is still a cold and desolate place.

See, I woke up this morning needing coffee like it was oxygen. Being an idiot, I had rung in 2000 at the bar, mixing cheap sparkling wine with beer, and rye and gingers. What was I thinking? And what was I doing out on New Year's Eve anyway? It's nothing but a friggin' Amateur Night, when every arsehole under the new moon thinks he can drink like Bukowski and stay as sharp as F. Scott. What the fuck do they know? Just a bar full of kids slurping their florescent martinis and whooping it up at the stroke of midnight like each chime really marked the beginning of something brave and new.

So I wake up, still fully clothed and stinking like the old, dead year, and drag my carcass out of bed to head to the doughnut shop. Christ. When I hit the street I'm blindsided by the ferocity with which winter lunges for my soft throat. Wind and ice slash at me — 1,000 broken bottles in the hands of 1,000 howling drunks. Shit, I've been living here all my life and every year the cold still catches me by surprise, still drags me into an alley and beats the tripe out of me. But I'm too stupid to remember to stay holed up until spring, and too dirt poor to move to some distant place with a Spanish name, where even the adobe bricks have been baked into usefulness by the sun.

Instead, I find myself leaning so hard into the storm's teeth that I don't see the sidewalk is blocked. I stumble over something and trip arse-over-tit. Because my hands are scavenging hopelessly for a wisp of warmth among the lint in the pockets of my thin jacket, I am unable to break my fall. My face slams hard into the cement, chipping an already snaggled tooth and splitting a nasty gash over my one good eye.

Lying there like a sack of freeze-dried turds, I swivel my head to see what pile of trash had ambushed me. I look dead into the marble eyes of a dead man. A bum. Blue and bloodless, his fat tongue stuck to the sidewalk by a delicate lattice of frozen saliva.

Now, I've seen a dead man on the sidewalk before, some old Hassidic guy getting run over by a heart attack on the front steps of a mall, but I *know* this bearded corpse. Not by name, but I can put a raspy voice to those chapped lips.

See, I used to work in a restaurant a mile down the road. Started off washing dishes and soaking bugs off lettuce in sinks full of water and vinegar. Eventually, I worked my way up to kitchen manager. The title sounds more important than the job really was. I still manned the grill during lunch rushes and swabbed out the toilets at night. All that changed was that I also had to make the schedules for the half-starved students who worked there and skew the inventory enough so that they could sneak an extra meal without us all getting fired.

One night at the end of my shift, I was hauling a bunch of charred brochettes to the garbage out back when I startled a bum hanging half in our dumpster. He was leaning in head-first with his shoes dangling in the air and I could hear him chewing on something crunchy. When the door slammed shut, he scrambled to his feet with a yelp and slunk toward the sha-dows of the parking lot.

He was tall and gangly and his oily jeans were a good six inches too short. Hunger and survival had etched their sto-ries in the lines in his face and in his prematurely grey beard, lips and skin. All the colour had been wrung right out of this guy for good.

"Hey," I called. He looked back at me with the same eyes you see on dogs who've been beat with sticks — and with good reason. I knew the other cooks in the area and some of them were real leather asses who'd like nothing more than to take out their minimum-wage frustration on this old bone rack. Down at Hell's Kitchen, Sanchez kept a knotted exten-sion cord by the backdoor so he could lash at down-and-out backs bent over the mouldy remains of a Greek omelette. San-chez was a sadist, a Mexican Captain Bligh. "Nobody eats for free," he'd hiss over beers, like some cold-blooded snake pressed between hot desert rocks.

Now I'm saddled with a hundred and one faults, including manic drunkenness and the crushing depression of sobriety, but beating the half-dead into a state of wholeness wasn't my bag. "Hey," I yelled again. "I ain't going to hurt you." He kept going though, not running, but not really walking. His eyes never left me. "Lemme get you some real food. You're just going to be digging it out of there afterward." I pointed to the dumpster. It was alive with fat, green-bodied flies reclaiming the feast that the bum had abandoned. He stopped and sized me up, gauging whether the risk was worth it. I did the same. I could tell that he was OK, a stray, for sure, but not yet rabid. Not yet bit by the werewolf.

My grandpa said I had a way with beasts. As a boy, I spent a summer on his farm. He was a good grandpa because he didn't buy into all that bullshit about forging a kid's character with hard labour. No early morning cow-milking or end-of-day hay-baling for me. Instead, he just let me be to explore his world by myself.

Mostly, I'd hang out with the animals. I liked the cows and horses well enough, but I was particularly drawn to the barn cats. They were as close as I'd ever come to wild animals — skinny little things that stayed alive on crickets and field mice and baby birds that fell from the nest too early. All my burly uncles said those cats could never be tamed, that they'd sooner claw my eyeballs out than fill my lap with purrs.

But my uncles were wrong. Took me two weeks of patience and a cupboard full of canned tuna to finally earn the cats' trust. By the end of August, all I had to do was stand on the porch and say *"pssst pssst pssst"* and 11 feral cats would materialize from the long grass to make nice with my ankles. "You're a regular Dr. Doolittle," grinned Uncle Stan. "You really speak their language, boy." Even back then I knew that language had nothing to do with it. If an animal is hungry enough, it will always take the risk.

Back in the kitchen, I slapped together a quick hamburger and fries for the old bum. He was standing there when I got back, the allure of fresh food was too much. Smiling, I held out the plate to him. "Mustard and relish, OK?" He grinned and took the plate. "Got any sweet pickles?" he asked.

By the time I had got back with the pickles the plate was empty. He slipped the green serrated slices into his mouth one at a time like they were slabs of smoked salmon. "That's a good pickle," he smiled. "A real fine pickle."

The hot food seemed to reanimate him, like a drowned swimmer on the end a lifeguard's lips. Pleased with himself, he puffed up his chest, and began pacing back and forth. Four strides east, four west. He started mumbling to himself in short, laughing bursts. His words came out machine-gun fast and I had trouble catching what he was on about, something about playing pianos, the Hollywood Fondas and the sky.

Pacing faster and faster, he rolled gibberish off his tongue like water off a waterfall. I had no clue what the sweet fuck this nut was rattling on about so I just leaned back and watched. Then, suddenly, he stopped dead and looked me square in the peepers. "Trinidad, my friend," he said slow and deliberate, Moses coming down from the mountain. "That's paradise, you know? That's where we're all gonna end up one day. Down there where it's hot and sandy and you can lie on the beach all day and dream till you're full. You can get fat on nothing but the sun down in Trinidad."

"Ever been?" I asked, curious as to who this guy was in his pre-dumpster days. Christ, that spooked him. His face, open and bright just moments before with the infinite promise of Trinidad, clouded over. He stared at me with his mouth slightly open and trembling, like he had an answer but that too many years of lonely monologue had stripped him bare of his ability to dialogue. My question opened the door to possible interaction, but his eyes looked scared, like I was coming at him with a bridle. Domestication terrifies all wild things.

The bum wheeled on his heel and bolted down the alley, the soles of his worn leather shoes chattering at me in retreat. "Hey," I yelled. "My plate, asshole. I need my plate." The next day I went out back for a smoke and the plate was sitting on the fire escape, clean as can be.

But that bum's not savouring sweet pickles any more. He's dead and bottlenecking my supply line to the doughnut shop. We're lying there, face to face in the snow. His eyes are black and without horizons, the same eyes you see on red snapper on ice down at the IGA. My first feeling is pity. "Poor bastard," I think in the smug, solemn way the living always lord it over the dead.

But the more I look at him, the more I feel something bad telling me that maybe he really isn't so different from me. Sure, my luck has run better than his, but probably not by much. And, yeah, I might have had more hot meals and bus passes and IKEA bookshelves than him but in the end it's just a thin screen that separates the two of us, no? A flip of the coin here, a troublesome recessive gene there — a lot of little things turned on him to throw the scales of natural justice out of whack. Things that could just as easily turn on me.

It frightens me how familiar his face is to me. I see it every-day. At the bar, in lines at the supermarket, holding up the hats of cops and construction workers, and, mostly, looking out at me from my mirror. Just another worn-down bastard going toe-to-toe against the freeze, slugging it out with invisible fears and trying to keep night from creeping in forever.

Christ, who isn't hungry for something? Love, religion, a sense of purpose. He just pared down that pang to its most elemental state. Even though I eat three squares a day, my insides have been hollowed out for years, no guts left in me at all. The only difference between this guy and me is that he's been worn down first. But I'll be there soon enough. You, too. Keep moving, people, keep moving or the cold'll get you. Or the heartache, or the taxman, or Sanchez, or the pointlessness of another sunrise. Another millennium.

And crazy as he was, at least this bum had that dream occasionally busting from the clouds to fill this grey winter landscape with a swatch of Caribbean sunlight and colour. I'm not so sure I can offer the same. A man's gotta have faith to dream because dreaming is the biggest risk of all.

I lie there, dragging my tongue over the new jag in my incisor and I let the warm piss of blood punch hot red bullet holes in the snow. Me and him, just a pair of poor saps desperately hunting for someone warm to stay alive against and maybe stretch this whole thing out till we get it right. Another day. Another week. Hoping to cling till spring, then get fat on sunny summer gravy. Happy New Year to you, chum, I think. A small ice pellet tornado swirls by us and the freeze crawls up my ass and burrows into my guts. This is a cold that will never leave.

I think about what my grandpa told me years later when I was no longer a boy and he came to pick me up at the airport in his truck. He told me how, a few winters after my stay on the farm, they had a record-breaking cold snap one night. When he went to the barn the next day, he found all 11 cats curled together looking like sleeping angels. They were dead, of course, and even though I had become a man, I still looked at grandpa for words of comfort, for the words to reassure me that the universe was unfolding as it should. But grandpa, the wisest and kindest man I ever met, had none. He just shrugged sadly at my teary eyes, the last vestige of childhood innocence. "The world is mean as hell, boy," he said, leaning over to snap my seat belt into place. "You'd better buckle up."

But grandpa is long gone and today I'm shivering in the snow beside an iced-over wild man who I once fed. Burger and pickles. Damn fine pickles.

The wind jumps, cuffing me in the back of the head. A man with a briefcase bustles up and strides two hurdler's steps over the wounded and the dead, and the world takes another half-turn creak on its icy axis. Reaching out, I snap the frozen spit anchoring the bum to this bitter here and now and pray that his next stop will be a warm one.

Shuffle Demons

Man, I remember that office job. It wasn't anything special, just regular paper shuffling stuff. Tough on the arse and fucking lethal for the creative spirit. Nothing throttles a man's inner muse with as much cold-hearted, sniper-in-the-bell-tower precision as paperwork. Fill in the blanks and file away the documents one day, and the next, your "In" box was heaped as high and shitty as Hercules' stables. It was like that *I Love Lucy* episode with the out-of-control conveyor belt full of bonbons.

But I schemed a system that worked like migrant Mexicans for me. Every morning I just shuffled all those nasty old papers straight into my trash can and by 10 a.m., I was killing the rest of the day flirting with the honeys down at the cafeteria and blowing imaginary smoke rings in the air.

It was a sweet gig. I'd lean up against the milk dispenser and grin at the office gals as they click-clicked their high-heels past me, a cavalcade of rounded calves and thighs. The Parade of Champions before the Kentucky Derby. I'd whip off some kissy-kiss poems on napkins and press them into talented 70-words-a-minute hands. Next thing you know, I was scoring furtive smiles from dark-eyed beauties and landing dinner dates that ended with long, luxurious, red-lipped desserts.

Nothing like screwing the women you work with. Above all else, they are wonderfully hung up on making sure no one else knows. It's a question of decorum. "Your secret is safe with me, baby," I'd Valentino into their ears and pat their plump rumps reassuringly. So hush-hush that none of the other women every found out. No jealousy. No scenes. No cat fights. Just pure, skin-covered bliss.

At my peak, I was playing a string of four ladies at the same time (three secretaries and a filing clerk) and no one was the wiser. "This is the first time I've ever been involved with a co-worker," I'd grin into their lusting, trusting eyes. "Normally I would *never* do this, but I knew there was some special back-and-forth happening between us." Then I'd roll them on top of me and start wiggling them around until we got the fire started.

They ate it up like bears on berries. What the hell, nothing like a secret office romance to fight the workaday crush. Might as well have been oxygen, we all needed it so bad. From 9-5 we'd sit there passively while our vital energies were wasted and drained, but at night, sonofabitch, me and the gals would wriggle and buck like life itself was on the line. We would recapture the flag that the straw bosses had stolen from us.

That's what it's all about isn't it? That's what screwing or fucking or making love or whatever the hell you want to call it, is all about, right? Life. No, not making life. Any frigging dung beetle can procreate. I'm talking about the struggle against death, in our case, the slow but inexorable demise of joy and creativity. Work'll carve your heart out and replace it with a punch clock. *Tick, tick, tick,* three seconds further from the soaring thrills of childhood, three seconds closer to some sombre, and distinctly adult end.

But nothing thumbs its nose at joylessness more than that final slippery lurch across the sexual finish line. Raises our sweaty, earth-bound bodies for a momentary swoop through heaven so we can snap our towels at the arses of those poor, chaste angels.

After all, sex is the essence of all we do, no? The god-damned sweaty centre of our beings. The raw, unthinking physicality and animal joys that bring divine release. Sex begins with us on the ground, huffing and crashing like engines and beasts, but where does it end? The sky. Heaven. The stars. I worship it for all its dark details, all its sweet tastes and mysterious sounds, all its nips and smells and hoarse pledges of forever. Let the Viking bastards keep Valhalla, my heaven is nestled between my lover's round thighs.

Yeah, yeah, I'm aware that there's lots more to life than love and sex. There's that first slice of sun pushing its way through your window every day. The unspeakable relief of letting ice-cold beer slide down your throat to wash away the trail dust and bitter insecurities. There's the smell of grilled cheese and bacon and the sound of good neighbours laughing behind bad apartment walls. But sex and love are the sum of all these things. It's the closest any of us get to great dance or song or poetry. Face it, we are, by and large, without grace in the way we lead our daily grind. But in bed, my love, ah! That's where we are Mozart.

But while I was busy composing great, sweaty operas between my sheets, all the other shuffle demons I worked with just kept getting more drawn and gaunt. The job was killing them with creeping malice. Each document was an 8.5 by 11-inch vampire that was sucking the life right out of them, drop by red drop. Death by a thousand paper cuts.

Each God-sent day, they'd scuff their way into work hunched like an Arkansas chain gang. All they did was shuffle papers from sunrise to sunset, Monday to Friday. *Shuffle, shuffle, shuffle.* A cross between a Vegas dealer and Sisyphus. And each day their dragging shoes wore down a little more and their shoulders crumbled a little more and their backbones and bellies grew a little more soft. They were getting smaller and smaller, disappearing before my sex-filled eyes.

Me, on the other hand, I was thriving and getting fat. I was Popeye with a belly full of spinach and a mouthful of Olive Oyl. I sprang out of my bed every morning before my alarm clock crowed. I belted out Ethel Merman show tunes in the shower and I hopped into my clothes like I was on the boards of Broadway. My eyes were clear, my shoulders squared and my legs had the spring of a man who was getting his on a nightly basis.

My co-workers hated me.

They couldn't figure out why I wasn't fading into shadows like the rest of them. They couldn't fathom how I still smiled, how I still cracked wise, how I still greeted my heaped "In" box with a whoop and a soft-shoe jig. They thought I was Satan.

See, I knew the secret. I had seen the light. I had Ponce de Leon-ed onto the fountain of youth — and I wasn't sharing. No way. No goddamned way. Not with that sorry lot of pressed shirts and sensible haircuts. Not with millionaires or heads of state. Not with anyone. Not even Johnny fucking Unitas. This was my private gold mine and I was going to keep panning it until I was turning up nothing but limestone. It was a sweet time of sex and poetry and a cafeteria full of smiling female faces. In my grandfather's parlance, I felt like a silk-crapping sonofabitch.

Of course, in the back of my mind I knew I was playing a dangerous game. When it comes to love and gambling a man can roll along real swell for a time, with his horses running fast and his women running faster. But always remember this: inevitably Luck and Circumstance will conspire to drop one big steamer on your racing form and another between your sheets. Eventually all your miles of silk work just ends up stinking like another yard full of shit.

One day I finished filing my day's work by 9:45. I was ahead of schedule, which meant I could score a good perch before the 10 o'clock coffee breakers started jiggling down the game trail. My eyes narrowed like those of a big cat as he gathers his pouncing legs beneath himself.

But before I could make my break, a co-worker — an ass-kissing stub of soft tissue named Clarence — stuck his head over my partition and said that Killington wanted to see me in his office, pronto. Killington was the supervisor, a mean-spirited Frankenfucker with a big bald head that looked like a 100-watt bulb.

When I strode through the door I was greeted by a group of serious-looking bastards from head office sitting around a conference table. These guys were corporate assassins; I could see it in the blood-sport glint in their eyes. Craps. My gravy train had just derailed and it was plain to see that there would be no survivors.

"McVie, would you care to explain this to me," Killington sneered, as he held an alarmingly thick folder in the air. "Would you care to explain this to all of us?" His voice rose.

"Would you kindly give an explanation as to why you haven't filed a single report in the past three months?" I could feel red-hot hate glowing off the bulb.

I slouched in my chair and smiled. In many ways the condemned man is the most free. "Well, gentlemen," I said with a slight bow of the head. "I'm glad you all could make it. Unfortunately, my findings aren't good."

Brows knit and some of the suits looked at each other. Killington, that ball-less whelp, just got redder. "What the hell are you ranting about, McVie?" he hissed.

I straightened up. "My findings, Killington. My findings over the course of this study have proven that you are an incompetent and ineffectual manager and one who is wholly not suited for responsibility of this magnitude." I crossed my hands on the desk in front of me and tossed a wink to the goon closest to me.

If we had been alone Killington would have slit me open from nuts to noggin. I was making a mockery of his precious inquisition. Rage launched a flare up his spinal column and exploded in his eyes. "What are you talking about?" he sputtered. "We're here to discuss your incompetence. We're here to ask you why you haven't done a lick of work for the past three months. We're here to find out what happened to the hundreds of important files that disappeared once they entered your office." He jammed his face up into mine, Billy Martin on an ump. His spittle burned my cheek. "In short, McVie, we're here to fire your lazy fucking ass."

I shook my head slowly and with great drama, the compassionate executioner. "Or, Mr. Killington, are we really here to find out why it took you three goddamned months to realize all this?" His eyes got buggy. He tried to mumble something, but I cut the egg-headed rat off. "Three months and how many important files, Killington? How many missed opportunities for the company? How much lost revenue? How can you explain that, except that you were asleep at the switch."

I paused and looked him square in his bloodshot pinballs. "It was your watch, Killington, and you let the Indians sneak into camp and pork the women."

The good news is that, for whatever reason, they forced Killington to retire a few weeks later with partial benefits. The bad news is that they unceremoniously sacked my ass right there on the spot. No benefits. No gold watch. No cheesy going-away party. No last dip in the secretarial pool.

Two months later I met Clarence sitting on the subway swinging his sawed-off little legs like an overweight member of the Lollipop Guild. He said that productivity had improved enormously since my dismissal. "When Mr. Killington retired, I was promoted to supervisor. Straightened up the whole department. I implemented a series of checks and balances to make sure that, well, *you know*, never happens again. Since then everything's been running A-OK," he said, smug as a man whose legs don't touch the ground can get. "Of course," he whined, "there *was* that unexplained malaise that ran through the secretarial corps for a month after you left."

I leaned back in my seat and blew an imaginary smoke ring in the air.

Ghosts

My brother drove a cab in Montreal back in the 80s when he was between jobs. The problem was, Ralphie isn't really much of a people person. Ninety-five percent of the world pisses him off to no end, which was the primary reason the sullen bastard was between jobs in the first place.

But driving a taxi is about the worst job a loner like Ralphie could be saddled with. Every day you're chatted up by dozens of yakkers. You get everyone, every idiot that God churned out on His off-days; blind guys with dogs that reek like dead trout; aerobics instructors who chirp like manic birds even though they've Tae-Boed their way to obsession and tit-lessness; old men yammering on about leaky parts; and frazzled moms whining about the rising cost of broccoli while their little beasts grease down your upholstery with ice cream and snot.

The biggest pains-in-the-ass are the long-winded happy-hour drunks who lean forward between the seats and can grab your shoulder so they can pour poison in your earhole about the bar bitches they could have banged. They stink of booze and smoke and day's end frustration. Their whole adult life they've been told to work from 9-5, to eat lunch from 12-1, to get two-for-one pissed from 5-7. Round-eyed salarymen. Ties undone, collars open, they sweat like bulls plowing in a field — bursting to be released from a lifetime of double-breasted yokes and the clutch of their 2.7 children. A driver can't get away from these guys; their eyes are right on top of you, dead embers in your rear-view mirror. Twin points of black and bloodshot hate.

"You're blocking the mirror, pal," you grunt. "Slide it over." But it's no use. They don't listen. Their ears are still crammed with the drunken lies they've been bullhorning at women all night, wrongly believing that volume is all that's needed to elevate themselves above the din of other macho braggarts. They talk sports like they're your best high-school pal, telling you what our hockey team needs most is a big power forward like Cam Neely used to be for the Bruins, a guy who can throw the hip check and drop the gloves and pot 40 goals a season. No shit, you think, gritting your teeth, what team doesn't need a horse like that?

"I used to play Junior A," they con you. "Played with Mario Lemieux for a year." Oh yeah? But when you ask them what year that would have been they pretend not to hear you. Slouching back into the seat, they stare out the window and try to imagine what it would be like hopping over the boards with Mario, streaking up the ice with Mario, getting a pass from Mario, having Mario stick his face in theirs after they score and say "Nice goal, Dave." Just parking themselves in front of the net and letting that big, beautiful bastard bank one off their stick past the goalie, bounce one off their ass. Lazy fucks even daydream lazy.

Half the time they'll pass out in mid-ride. Like their bull-shit has its limits and by the time they get in your car, they've already used all but ten minutes of their daily quota. Their heads fall back, mouths open, unvoiced dreams and aspirations spilling into your car, soundlessly igniting upon re-entry into this brutal atmosphere. Dreams they didn't even know they had. You glide along to their place in silence, ghost-men in the street. Ghosts.

Then there are the students. They squeeze five of them in your car, forcing you to shuffle your newspaper and Halls mentholyptus cough drops from the front seat to make room. Five of them, and they still have to pool coins for a seven-buck ride. Fifty-cent tip, maybe.

Sometimes they're out-of-towners, spoiled little shits from Boston up on a bus excursion paid for by MIT daddy. And it's always the jerky one who sits next to you. The fat boy in an old Ray Bourque jersey, the one with an earring sticking out of his face. Another one of life's bulls, shackled to the rest of the non-conformist herd by the ring in his nose. He thinks it's a state-ment, but the statement is "I'm with them." He's the worldly one who likes to strike up a conversation with you man-to-man. The other pimple faces smirk from the shadows when he asks you where the strippers and hookers hang out. And because you despise the Bruins, you drop the whole bean-eat-ing crew off on St. Catherine and St. Laurent where, my brother likes to say, the strippers put their teeth *in* before they go to work and the hookers take them *out*.

Yeah, Ralphie hated that cab. Hated it like rot. So, I used to earn some spare coin driving it around. I'd give him a few bucks from whatever I earned. I guess he was like a pimp, but what did it matter? I was too lazy to get registered and I needed to kill the nights when sleep wouldn't come easy.

Once in late October, I get dispatched to an address in Point St. Charles. I know the Point well because that's the neigh-bourhood where my old man grew up. People may tell you that it's getting all chichi-fied and done up nice, but that's only along the canal.

Sixty years ago, the old waterway was a major industrial artery, lined with machine shops and abattoirs. Now yuppie artists and software developers nest there, feng shui-ing in lofts where man and beast once were slaughtered, sometimes mercifully quick, sometimes over the course of a plodding life-time. But just south of the canal, hidden from view behind the protective and picturesque treeline, it's still just a neighbour-hood of Irish-style row houses and shiners and wary cats limp-ing through alleys that sparkle with broken glass.

I pull up to the address and idle, but no one comes out. When I honk the horn a saw-toothed kid scowls at me from the stoop across the way. My dad had the same trust-nobody scowl. Dropped a nurse with a right cross for coming at him with an enema two weeks before we buried him. He was a real red-ass even at 78 with barely any heartbeat in him.

The curtain flutters and the porch light flicks on. Dusk was settling like dirty river silt. The door opens and a bald head pokes out. A hand waves at me to come over. Christ, must mean luggage. Some poor old-timer going for his annual $50 bus ride to Lake Memphremagog or something.

When I walk over, the door is ajar. I push it open and find a bent little man in his 80s screwing a wide-brimmed fedora into place on his head. His tiny bird body is draped in an equally tiny camel-haired coat. It looks as ancient as him, but in good condition. The old folks in the Point are like that; they're potato-famine poor, but they all have one good set of clothes saved for funerals and weddings and trips to Lake Memphremagog.

He smiles and waves me over, "Come in, come in." Two large suitcases wait for me. The day's dying light reveals two small rooms with sheets covering the furniture and throw rugs rolled up like threadbare cigars. The yellowing walls are bare and a few open boxes contain framed black-and-white photographs. A small dish sits on the hallway floor crusted with cat food, but there is no cat in sight.

"Could you help me with one of these, son?" he asks, trying to drag one of the bulky suitcases toward the door. I shake my head and grab them both. I've always pitied men who outlive their strength.

As I'm loading the bags into my trunk, I watch him shuffle unsteadily along the walk. A mime's robot. I'd laugh out loud if his face weren't so concentrated on keeping the shuffle moving forward. I lend him my elbow and lead him to the car. He weighs nothing on my arm, barely a hint of a person. Before he dips his fedora into my cab, he surveys the street and waves at the black-browed boy, telling him to be good. The kid waves back and smiles as if kissed by prosperity and love. A momentary respite from the scowling rest of his life.

The old man gives me the address and asks if we go via downtown. I tell him it's the long way around, that it would tack five bucks extra on the meter. "That's all right, son," he says. "I'm on my way to a hospice. I'm in no hurry."

We drive in silence for a few minutes before he tells me that the doctors hadn't given him much time. The cancer had settled in for good. I say I'm sorry and I mean it. Cancer hollowed out my ma years ago and it's a shitty way to go. "Thank you," he replies "but it's time. I don't have anyone left anymore."

He tells me where to turn, giving me a running commentary as we roll up and down the streets. "I first met my wife, Margaret, right over there," he says, pointing to a hairdressing salon. "Except, back then it wasn't much more than a field where the police ran their horses. She loved sneaking them sugar cubes and scratching them along the jaw, just under the ears. Got to the point where they'd come trotting over like dogs whenever she called." His voice is light with those memories. Happy.

We pass the squat apartment block where he and Margaret first made their home after he came back from the fighting overseas. "No hot water in that one," he chuckles. "No ice box either. In winter, we'd keep our perishables out in the shed in an old chest so the squirrels and mice wouldn't get at them."

"How 'bout in the summer?"

"We just ate faster," he said with a wink.

Further uptown he shows me the old printing press where he worked as a typesetter, and he dangles his still-stained fingers over my seat as proof. His fingertips touch my shoulder. They are thin and delicate like I'd imagine you'd find on a concert pianist. Old people always look so cold to the touch, like their blood doesn't move too far out from their heart for fear that it might never find its way back. Not this old fellow, though; even through my thick sweatshirt I can feel the warmth emanating from his hand.

"Rockhead's," he smiles when we reach the corner of St. Antoine and Mountain. My father used to crow about what a great club Rockhead's was before the wrecking ball obliterated it in the name of progress. He'd tell me how all the great black entertainers would play there back when Montreal was one of world's premiere towns. "We saw Sammy Davis Jr. dance there one night," the old man says. "Long before he was a big star with Sinatra. Saw Ella Fitzgerald there, Nina Simone and the great Dinah Washington."

His eyes are on me in the rear-view and so is his smile. For a good long while he holds my gaze and I can see him and Margaret all decked out and snapping their fingers to Basie's band and Dizzy's be-bop. Outside, people scuttle by, entirely unaware of the corner's place in history. But the car is brimfull with it.

You know, sometimes you need a guy like him in the back of your cab. Someone talking good about his life and good about his people. A decent man made decent not by scoring Cup-winning goals or thrusting an Oscar into the Hollywood air. Just a man who lived right, who did it well while nobody was looking. Listening to him, I feel about as good as I can get while I'm not on the bottle. Even Ralphie would have liked this old gent.

We drive around for an hour, but I had turned off the meter long before. He tells me all kinds of stories. Stories about him earning nickels as a pin boy in a bowling alley and working his way up to copy editor at *The Gazette*. Then there was his ill-fated stint as a bantamweight boxer. "The boys at the gym called me Kid Candle — one blow and I was out," he laughed. He wasn't put here to fight, I think, not with gentle hands like that.

He tells me he saw Jackie Robinson playing up here for the Montreal Royals the year before he signed on with Brooklyn. Says he was one of the hundreds of men who huzzahed after Jackie when he won the Little World Series for us. "The papers wrote that it was the first time in history a black man ran from a white mob that had love on its mind," he chuckles. "And I do believe they were right."

He talks about war and love and about the friends who'd gone on before him, holding out details of other people's lives like they were polished gemstones. Every small story is stand-alone perfect, paying final unembellished tribute to a simple life lived grandly.

Eventually he directs me to Mount Royal Cemetery and I park in the near-empty lot. He's come to see Margaret one last time. I open the door for him and guide him out into the night. He doesn't have to ask. I give him the crook of my arm and we shuffle down the path; row after row of headstones and silence.

"Here we are," he says and cuts himself free of me, preferring to walk the last ten feet under his own steam. He dodders around the simple plot, fussing with a bouquet of plastic flow-ers and whisking away stray leaves with his toe. He reaches out for the tombstone with his shaking printer's hand.

Margaret Delaney 1920-1994
Hold me but safe again within the bond
Of one immortal look

His fingers grip the corner for balance, but his thumb rubs back and forth across the rough face out of love. Skin on stone, a caress almost too small to be seen.

We stand there for ten minutes. Sometimes his lips move, but no sounds come out. I don't need to hear to know that he is mouthing words of devotion and the promise of reunion.

"I think we should go now," he finally says without tak-ing his eyes off the headstone. "I'm getting tired." He kisses his fingertips, presses them onto the top of the marker and reaches out for me. We walk back to the car without talking, the bone-rattle of bare branches the only sound in the world.

I drive him to the hospice, a big efficient building of brown brick and mortar. Looking up at the small, uniform windows, I picture him sitting behind one of them, locked in his cell. Waiting for it to come. As soon as we pull up to the entrance two orderlies bustle out like they had been expecting the old man a long time ago. By the time I haul his bags from the car they've already got him belted in a wheelchair.

"How much do I owe you, son?" he asks.

"Nothing," I say standing above him. "It's on the house."

"That's no way to run a business," he protests, leaning back and reaching into his coat pocket.

"They'll be other fares," I say. I put my hand on his shoulder and he stops his search.

"God bless you," he smiles.

"Yeah. God bless you, too."

He sandwiches my big hand in his small ones and pats it. "He already has, son. A whole lifetime of blessings."

The orderlies wheel him away and the automatic doors shut behind him with a hiss, the sound a person makes as they slip through life's fingers. Another ghost off the street and onto the loading dock. The last thread linking the lives of friends and family, doing them honour and keeping them alive with love and story.

Weddings, baptisms, battles along the Rhine, midnight bonfires lighting up the streets in Point St. Charles, Ella's unrecorded concerts, newspaper headlines, Jackie rounding third and digging for home, Margaret on his lips, boating along the canal; who would be their keeper now? An old man's memories, an old man's life, waiting to unravel with a last breath.

Getting back into my cab I notice that he has forgotten something in the back seat. A black-and-white photograph in a simple pewter frame. A wedding photo of a small, trim man in uniform linking arms with a smiling woman with dark curling hair. Sixty years of poverty stretched out before them, but they are happy and in love, and it is plain to see in the way they are looking at each other that, in this case anyhow, love will be good enough.

I almost bring the picture back to the old man, but I wonder what will happen to it when he dies? With no friends or family to claim it, the photo will undoubtedly be thrown out. Incinerated. Instead, I bring it back to my apartment and make room for it in the middle of a cluttered shelf. I will keep it. I will be its keeper.

Zeke

I knew this guy named Zeke from down at the bar. Zeke was a plumber who owned his own company. He'd come for a few beers at the end of another week of washers and elbow joints. Frenchie, the bar historian, claimed that Zeke was a shit-hot high-school baseball star who got a crack in the minors before he blew a knee trying to stretch a double into three. He was a slugging centerfielder and they said he could jack the ball like Mantle.

Every week Zeke would come banging through those doors smiling and shaking hands and grabbing us by the back of our grimy necks in a real friendly fashion. He was a swell guy. Straightforward and generous, he'd always buy rounds for the gang on big holidays, even during stretches when people's drains were staying unclogged and their pipes were running drip-free.

The girls were always slinking up and squeezing in on him because he had those square shoulders and Popeye forearms. But Zeke would just wink at the whispered propositions and say, "Aw hell, Martha, you're gonna make me blush again." And, sure enough, he'd go red as rust.

There were a lot of women who'd have gladly taken some of Zeke's part-time loving. Gladly have wrapped their lust around him an afternoon here or there. But Zeke wasn't like that. He was a family man, always cutting out a little early so he could buy a bag of candies for his kid or stop by the flower shop and get a bouquet of daisies for his wife, Daisy. "Thank Jesus she isn't named Rose, or I'd be broke," he'd chuckle.

Yeah, Zeke really loved that wife and kid of his. He always had new stories about his son. "The Boy is learning how to bunt," he'd tell us and we'd all nod and smile and tell him to make sure The Boy didn't jab at the ball with the bat. Not when you're bunting, no way.

And our smiles were sincere — a rarity for that lot — because Zeke's love and pride was infectious. "The Boy's team won their division yesterday," he'd crow and a roomful of drunks and dead-enders would slap backs and whoop it up like The Babe had clobbered number 60.

One day The Boy, not yet ten, was hanging out at the end of his street with some friends, tossing around a football in an old lot. The trouble was, at the end of the lot there lived a Bad Guy. A drug-pushing Bad Guy.

On top of having a parade of scumbags and crack sluts filing in and out of his digs every day, the Bad Guy had three killer dogs. I was told that they were all some kind of pit bull mix raised on bloody ground beef and cigarette burns. All I know is that when the Bad Guy walked that slobbering trio down the street it made me think about Cerberus. Which would make that house Hades.

While the kids are horsing around, the football gets punted into the Bad Guy's yard and The Boy hops over the chain-link fence to retrieve it. The dogs come howling out of their plywood lean-to and tear into him, ripping out his groin and throat. By the time the Bad Guy beats back his monsters, The Boy — Zeke's boy — is dead.

His friends go running and screaming to Zeke, who, in turn, limps full speed down the street on his bad leg only to find his son laid out on the sidewalk, torn open like a chicken. The Bad Guy hasn't even called an ambulance because he's freaking out trying to dispose of all his drug shit before the cops get there.

Zeke cradles The Boy's skinny body, carries him back home, and lays him out on his bed surrounded by posters of sports heroes and kung fu movie stars. Then Zeke goes to the closet and gets his baseball bat — a Louisville slugger, Roger Maris model — and walks back down the street to Hades.

He kicks open the gate and kills every dog in the yard, including two rottweilers who were just parked there while their owner helped the Bad Guy sanitize his house. Even dogs can be in the wrong place at the wrong time.

Zeke got bit, mind you. He got bit real bad in the hand and leg. But he didn't feel the pain, he just kept swinging for the fences. Dead dogs everywhere. They didn't have a fucking chance — not against a Double A swing that sweet.

Just as Zeke is icing the fifth and final dog, the owner of the rotts comes out and finds my man all covered in blood and brain and bits of fur. This guy has no goddamned clue who Zeke is, and he's not about to stand around and play Twenty Questions. He reaches for a shiny gun in his belt, but never gets it drawn. Zeke drops the meaty part of the bat on the guy's melon and splits it wide. Easier than the fucking dogs.

He tears inside like a murderous storm cloud and catches the Bad Guy by surprise. Shatters his kneecap with one malicious chop. Zeke goes about pulverizing the guy's legs and arms and hands and elbows in the meanest, most methodical way. I mean, the Bad Guy is pulp, he can't even raise his hands to protect himself. All he can do is cower in the corner and get hammered to sawdust like the heavy bag down at the gym.

Bang. Zeke caves in the fucker's teeth and slams his jaw halfway around his head, but somehow the poor bastard doesn't pass out. He just lies there wailing and oozing blood, tears, snot and thick mucous beaten from the darkest parts of his guts. Neighbours say his screams tore open the sunny summer sky.

Sirens start getting real close. Zeke digs in one last time, raises that 34-ounce piece of polished ash high over his head and drives the Bad Guy out of Hades and straight to Hell.

Zeke should have got a medal and the key to this fucking city for what he did. Instead, he got free room and board for 25 years in a barb-wired hotel. Stupid fucker. Why would he do that? Giving up his handsome wife and his once-a-week beer and his twice-a-week lay and his business and his laughter and his baseball trophies, for what? Revenge? Retribution? Justice? Misguided motherfucker. Now all he's got to cling to are his wife's brave smiles on the other side of the Plexiglas sheet and a wall of curled photographs.

Somebody should have let Zeke in on the secret: there is no justice. Not in this time, not in this civilization. Jesus wasn't the first poor bastard to die pinned to a cross, and he certainly won't be the last. No, now we elect crack smokers and sex perverts and reward murdering athletes with freedom and fat paychecks and adulation. The honest men get buried away, buried alive for good. What kind of chance does a plumber with a gimpy knee have against a stacked deck like that?

I keep meaning to go down and visit Zeke. You know, wish him well and tell him that the gang is thinking about him. But I never seem to get around to it. Guess I prefer to remember him like he was when he was still alive.

Honey-Tongued Hooker

Yesterday I passed a fourteen-year-old hooker by the Dunkin' Donuts. Maybe fifteen. She had shoe-horned her little boy ass into a pair of white tights that looked like they were peeled off a Barbie doll. This baby slut was no Barbie doll, though. No fucking way. Barbie has healthy pink skin and big blue eyes painted on an unblemished face. This tramp was all glazed and bloodshot. Her eyes hung heavy on her face.

But there was something happening back there behind the 1,000-cock stare. Thinking back to sunny times on the farm? School-yard days playing Red Rover with her friends and being teased by freckle-faced boys? Maybe. But I doubted it. I figured she wasn't thinking much beyond getting a batch of forgetfulness stuck in her arm or up her nose, or reeling in another two-legged meal ticket. Talk about a daily grind.

"Wanna date, honey?" she asked in a little voice as I passed. Honey? I hadn't been called that since I was a kid mugging around at the motel pool run by one of my dad's friends. In summertime, dad would hold court on a lawn chair surrounded by his cronies, the whole mob of them squeezed into Speedos and wrapped in alligator boot flesh. Just sizzling in the heat like happy iguanas on Galapagos. The women could have been movie mobsters' wives: dyed blond hair stacked high and hard; sunglasses that got bigger each year to hide crumbling eyes and once-sharp cheek bones; and wired-up leopard bathing suits that creaked beneath the prodigious weight of migratory bosoms.

They'd sit there day after day, summer after summer, faces turned in reverential sacrifice toward the sun — the last of their Valentinos not yet lured away by the transient mysteries of younger, firmer sirens. They coated themselves with oil, gobs of buttery lube. Basting like big-titted turkeys, complete with gobbler necks and heavy brown drumsticks.

The pool was a treat for me and my brother. We'd spend all day in the water, wrestling, swimming, holding our breaths, pissing in the shallow end — all that stuff that ices a kid's cake. When we got wrinkly and blue-lipped, we'd wrap ourselves in towels and worm ourselves in beside dad. The conversation among he and the boys was always the same, shit-funny slags being tossed around and someone recounting the previous night's misadventures. They all used swear words like punctuation marks, and I revered them because they never changed the way they spoke when us kids skittered over. No rolling eyes or whispered pig Latin. I felt like I was privy to their secret, exciting world. I felt like an adult. Scooched there beside my big, laughing dad and spun up in my terry-towel chrysalis I was taught the invaluable lessons of humour and friendship and the community of men.

The wives sat in their gaggle on the outskirts of the sacred ring of lawn chairs chatting and scolding each other's brats. Every now and then they'd rattle their ice at me. "Honey," they'd yodel, "be a sweetheart and fetch me a rum and coke. Tell Sam to put it on Dutch's tab." Entranced by their conical breasts, I'd nod a dutiful yes and go water-bugging to the bartender. Sometimes I'd steal a sip on my way back. On those really sweet, sweaty days, when the sun hung up forever and the entire crew was there, I'd have a good little buzz going by the end of our stay. Hazy memories of warm summer days.

But this was no warm day at the pool and this teenage ass-merchant was about 40 summers short of calling me honey. I stopped. She slipped out of the doorway and barged her tiny body into my open jacket. She repeated her offer, "Wanna date?" I instinctively shifted away from her, but she pressed her advantage inward. Her head was at my chest and her bloodless fingers brushed my hips. Those damaged blue eyes looked through me to the promise of a brief interlude from winter's street corner.

She pushed up against me, pushed soft but persistent. They hardly moved at all, but her searching fingers felt like they were looking to trigger the latch to a secret door. Like she was standing in the claustrophobic antechamber just a wall away from spacious breathing rooms. Her liquid hands poured across my body's bumpy surface, seeping into each crevice and filling them with something more than just quiet desperation. I thought of a blind man lost in a cave or a swimmer trapped under lake ice, pressing up against the hard surface and squeezing into every hollow to claw at the bitter promises hiding in the cracks.

Except this girl wasn't looking for a way out, she wanted in. The good whores learn how to read a man in seconds so they can tailor their pitch appropriately and lay the right bait. Nice Guy, Shy First-Timer, Protector, Hound Dog, Mean Fucker; they have all our angles covered. This kid repulsed me in a real primordial way, like meat gone gag-sour in the summer, but something about her made me feel sorry, even guilty. And she sensed it, like a street dog smells fear, impaling herself —

almost gratefully, imperceptibly — on each sliver of empathy that jabbed out from my eyes. And she wriggled — more grateful than ever — on their tiny hooks. She wanted more from me than $75.

Maybe the banks of her childhood had eroded and fallen into this malicious river way too fast. I glimpsed the crying child standing among the levee's ruins as dark adult water swirled unabated around her legs, obliterating carefree, happy times. Spilled ink on a page. No gradual transition to help callus her up. No protective cocoon in which to sprout grownup legs and eyes and strong arms to beat back the beasts and whore masters. Suddenly there she was, the spent old hag in the little girl's shell, like those Russian dolls in reverse. The little one entombs the bigger one.

She pressed up inside me, up against my chest, squeezing in on my heartbeat and lungs. I felt her cat mouth sucking up my breath. Her thin-boned hands burrowed like small sparrows in the snow, digging deep into the cold to scavenge some warmth from my sunny memories. I let her stand inside me for a spell. We both needed it.

Did I feel juiced for sex? Fuck. Don't ask. Did I take her up on her offer? Did I feel the bitter zing of melancholy prick itself through my skin, ease straight into my vein and mix with my filthy, lusty blood? All of the above, friend. Intoxicating. Terrifying. But you have to believe me, I really wanted to take her somewhere else. A swimming hole. A country brook. A lake. The endless possibilities of oceans. I wanted to wrestle around in shallow water and splash her face and rub off the trashy paint. Wipe her slate clean. Soak her with cannonballs and hot seats and the inconsequential beads of compassion. Instead, I took her to a motel. I thought maybe they had a pool.

Fragile Birds

Kimmy was one of those gals that glide through a man's line of sight once a lifetime. If she was a deer and you were a hunter, you'd lay your rifle down forever and spend the rest of your life rooting around for tofu and grubs.

I couldn't stop loving her, even though that same love kept taking me outside and beating the snot out of me. She was tragedy and comedy all woven together in one dramatic masterpiece. Only she could make me laugh and scratch my head and pull tears from my dry eyes, all in the same five minutes. One moment I was up there, mighty Icarus, winging along with the high fliers, and the next I was watching the hard, blue ocean jumping up to pulverize my yellow bones to dust. Gals like her don't exactly spoil you for other women, they just prepare you for what Heaven must certainly be like. This is particularly wonderful for schmucks like me, who've never really planned on getting there in the first place.

I was bigger, stronger, more soulful for having had her in my life and in my art. And for having had her on my lips. *Today this heart is fat and happy* I wrote in a note that I left stuck on her bathroom mirror one morning. *Today seems like it could last forever.* It was a funny note for me because I've never been a forever kind of guy.

The first time I saw her, my heart hurt because it wasn't big enough for what I was feeling. Like the Grinch when he goes good. I won't cliché it all to hell by saying that my heart was bursting, but it sure as shit was squeezing out at my ribs.

It's the same feeling of elation that zinged through me only once before. I was bobbing along on a ferry off the coast of Ireland and five dolphins appeared out of nowhere to escort our boat. They darted into formation beside us, just an arm's length away, hanging in the air like glistening, muscular kites. Every time they'd leap from the water I could see their brilliant eyes looking right into mine, checking me out with that little dolphin grin. Wild, but full of fun, compassion and humanity. For the first time since I was a leaky-nosed kid I laughed out loud from pure joy. Just like that. Here, in my blacktop and steel neighbourhood we don't have too many encounters with wild animals, and that moment will be forever etched in my heart where all our best memories are held.

Of course, every day without the dolphins is another day without that soaring joy, another day of mediocrity and hand-to-mouth. A box X-ed out on the calendar. And every second without Kimmy is another moment that I must populate with the memories of love, or share with another woman altogether. Someone else's Kimmy, perhaps, but not mine.

I remember the first night we slept together — or at least snatches of it. Not surprisingly, I was hammered. She was pretty liquored herself, too drunk to climb behind the wheel of her rusty shitbox. Luckily, she was sober enough to steer me into my rat-hole apartment and guide me to my lumpy bed. I fell like a doomed redwood.

Once I finished bouncing, I looked up from the mattress and patted the spot beside me with the lecherous grin I had inherited from Uncle Mort. "Shit, woman. As long as I have a bed, you have a place to park your ripe arse."

She laughed and threw one of her shoes at me. Her drunkenness had steadied her aim — she clocked me right in the ear-hole. I threw my head back and yowled like a wolf in a leg trap. She laughed harder and flung her other shoe, narrowly missing me.

"Come on, sweet cheeks," I slurred. "How long are we going to circle each other like this?" A balled-up sock bounced off my nose. "It's in the cards for us to shack up for awhile. It's fated. I read it in my tea leaves this morning." Her other sock ricocheted harmlessly off my groin.

I couldn't take my eyes off her now naked feet. I felt my boxers bunch up. Her sweat pants winged by me and knocked the phone off my night table. Standing in her little black panties, she belly laughed some more, a laugh that rolled effortlessly out of the child's corner of her heart. Sounded like a county fair to me, a Ferris wheel. White linen snapping in summer's late day kiss.

Standing there, she was all lean legs with fine, spider webs of muscle running top to bottom. "Sweet child of light, you have million-dollar wheels," I whispered, slowly slipping off a shoe of my own.

Her T-shirt billowed through the air and landed gently on my face. I tilted my head forward and the shirt slipped onto the floor. There she sat in all her grinning, braless glory. My breath jumped out of my body, a battered welterweight taking one last jackhammer shot to the ribs. And I'll be damned if I didn't catch a whiff of the salty Irish coast.

The next morning, I woke up with Buddy Rich pounding "Sing, Sing, Sing" in my head. The young day's sun had slipped in through my grungy blinds and, like a secret lover, was caressing her in adoring silence. Little particles of dust floated through the beams of sunlight and shrouded her in soft focus magic. Ingrid Bergman saying goodbye on the runway. "Fucking fairy dust," I thought with awe. I sat upright in bed and leaned against the wall and it pressed cool into my back.

Her tight little body seemed so spare, as if it would tear like rice paper under my gaze. I could see her back rise with each breath, and I marvelled at the sublime beauty of each individual rib. She had been fashioned by God's own hands and it was plain to see that He must have taken extra loving care with her. There was no way He'd have trusted one of His heavenly underlings with creation that sweet.

And her ass. For a long time I just stared at her round ass and, suddenly, poetry happened in my heart. Poetry! It had been years since I had written poetry of any consequence, years since I had felt the desire or that gnawing need to write verse. But, when I looked at her ass poetry ran tin cups along my ribs and demanded release. I felt invisible hands slip the big iron key in the lock and give it a rusty turn.

Heart doing flip-flops, I snatched a pen and a piece of paper from the jumbled mess of my life that mostly lay scattered on the floor. Softly, gently and with reverence and religion and the beginnings of a hard-on, I placed that single sheet of paper on top of the white marble altar of her ass. I began to write.

Sated by sex and dance and booze, she didn't stir. And so, I just kept writing. At first it was just images, the seeds of poetry. Then it sprouted into lines and stanzas and heroic couplets and Shakespearean sonnets and elaborate open verse. I poured metaphysical allusions, personifications, metaphors, imagery, irony and symbolism onto that page, and somehow, inscribed them unseen onto her body. I could feel her pores soak up my words.

Just as the page rounded to her gently curving haunch, so too my verse wrapped itself around her pliable skin. So fucking organic. No hard edges against which the fragile birds of poetry would stun themselves when they fluttered free. Just the give-and-take of paper and warm flesh. Like writing on Polynesian water.

Granted not all of it was great poetry — some of it wasn't even very good — but I felt like a sprinter stretching his running legs after a long ride in a little car. Like a boxer working off the ring rust on the heavy bag. Like a celibate finally dropping it in. It felt good to flex my poetic muscles again.

"Ouch!"

In my zest, I poked through the page with my pen. Kimmy's sleeping ass sprang taut. The poetry screeched to a stop. "What the hell are you doing back there, McVie?" she whispered with a raggedy voice.

"Poetry, sweet cheeks!" I enthused as I kissed the small of her back. "I'm writing poetry! Now relax. Stop clenching your butt." I jiggled her cheek with a loving hand.

"Poetry?" She knew all about my poetic impotence, but her despotic hangover was too overbearing to grant her the luxury of enthusiasm. She plopped her head back onto the warm divot in her pillow. "That's great. Just watch your pen, OK?" Her muscles relaxed under my protective touch and the poetry flowed again.

For the next eight months that poetry flowed, so long as Kimmy would let me use her ass as inspiration and a desk.

Virtually every night that we were together I would get her to lie down and hike up her dress so that I could release the birds from their prison. The poetry that I wrote during that period eventually filled four volumes, including the award-winning *Asspirations*.

She thought the whole thing was crazy, but craziness was one of the things that most attracted her to me. "Aside from its really anal offshoots," she used to say with absolute sincerity, "insanity is marked by heavy sexiness."

And often the poetry did lead to sex. Fabulous fucking. Poetry and her naked haunches filled me with a monumental lust. Once she was lying there on her belly knitting while I scribbled away. Suddenly, I bellowed like a conquering animal and hurled my pen against the wall. Poem finished. "Couplets and coupling," I wailed like a call to arms as I straddled her.

Some mystic had once told her that her pelvis was like a cracked bowl. I immediately fell in love with the sad imagery and wanted to seal that melancholic crack with my mouth and healing breath. Wanted to echo my soothing words inside her body.

I drank from the bowl of her pelvis. Reached under her buttocks and lifted that sacred cup to my lips. One sip, one dizzying taste, brought me closer to God than all the gallons of sacramental wine I had sneaked as a wayward choirboy.

The moment begged the question: How could the Holy Spirit be contained more fully in a bottle of fruity red than in the body of such divine grace? "No wonder priests are all fucked up," I thought in a rare metaphysical moment. "Too much tasting of cheap wine and choirboys and just not enough pussy."

Of course I was probably over-simplifying the complex issues of devotion and sex and religious callings, but I didn't give a shit. If you stare at something long enough all the extraneous crap just falls away. All you are left with is the truth. How many truths could I discover staring at her? Hundreds? Thousands? Maybe an infinite number. I knew that it really didn't depend on her, she was all truths just waiting for me to uncover.

But she had Gaelic wild in her. A big, old troublesome river of wild jarring through her. Like a rich vein of gold slicing through a mountain. Kissing her was like standing on the strand of beach in Bantry Bay and feeling the Atlantic salting my lips and eyes and tongue in prelude to a storm.

Once, after sex, she lay back with her eyes closed and smiled. "McVie, I like you," she said in that raspy voice of hers. "You're soft and hard and fun in all the right places. Nothing halfway. I bet when you were little you were one of those kids who turned over rocks and moved the slugs around — switching them, then putting back the rocks. Me too. I bet we would have been raucous playmates." She laughed. "Can't imagine a little McVie. What a holy-rolly terror."

I thought back to when I was a blond-haired kid and wished I could have swapped slugs with Kimmy. Knowing me, I probably would have saved them as boyhood love tokens and carried them forever. Of course, it would be hard to explain to grown women how come my pockets rattled with dried slugs. Most women wouldn't understand the machinations of a little boy in love.

But like all good things in my life, our relationship was doomed to one of two fates: to fizzle beneath damp indifference or to crash and burn in colossal tragedy.

Eventually the poetry writing ritual started wearing a little thin for Kimmy. I grew increasingly obsessed by it. I always wanted to write. The sex stopped. She would try to wiggle her ass to entice me as I wrote, but it just frustrated me. "Stop yer wiggling," I would huff and dot an "i" with extra malice.

She would fart her revenge at me.

My poetry was getting big and intense. It was complex and ornate, like wrought-iron railings and grillwork in New Orleans. Sure, it was bright and brilliant, but Kimmy was fading in its glare.

"I'm going to Vancouver tomorrow," she announced from her stomach one morning. "I'm going to stay with Marcy until I can get settled." I dropped my pen and watched stupidly as it rolled off her ass and tumbled to the floor in slow motion. I said nothing. No sobbing, no threats, no pleading, no questions. I had known all along that the fall was inevitable. "Too fucking close to the sun again," I thought. I could almost smell the melting wax.

Instead I removed the unfinished poem from her ass and gave each cheek a soft kiss. I lay my head upon her warmth and drifted to sleep. For the first time since I was a light-souled boy, I dreamed sweet dreams of flying with the swifts and swallows.

We slept like that for hours. When we awoke later that afternoon, she rolled out of bed and got dressed. I watched wordlessly as she shimmied her light summer dress past her shoulders, down her back and over that ass one final time. Like a curtain falling on a great fucking play. She kissed my lips and smiled sadly into my bloodshot eyes. Out the door forever.

Two poetry-free months later, I got a package in the mail from her. The scented note gave me incomplete glimpses into her life on the coast and reminded me of how much I really cared for her. Her voice, her laugh — all her sounds were in me now. In my ears. In my head. In *my* voice and *my* laugh and *my* sounds. In me for keeps. She signed the letter with a little sketch of me and her sitting at the bar belly laughing. She was a crappy artist, but a magical woman.

She had also enclosed a picture. A beautiful picture. A close-up of her naked ass. I stuck a thumb tack in the corner of the polaroid and jammed it into the gyprock wall over my desk. I turned on my computer, and as I waited for it to hum back to life, I felt the wingbeats of impatient poetry whisper along my ribs.

The Strip Joint
and the Tribal Tree

I'm in a strip joint sizing up the peelers. Fuck. Not real, these women. Flawless specimens with white teeth, high breasts and delicate blonde fuzz on hard, machine-tanned asses.

I don't belong to the same species. Me, with my short, squat body; more chimp than man. These ultra-women are the cartoon fantasies of my simian tribe. We huddle and hoot from the stale corners of the bar, red eyes ablaze with lust and the petty malice that marks our breed. A roomful of erections straining impotently against the dual bonds of pants and poisoned desire.

What do these false goddesses feel as they wiggle and jut? Mockery, perhaps. Physical perfection on stiletto heels, naked and beyond shame. Untouchable — and not just because the two brutes at the door are even greater apes than the rest of us.

We can only stare as the dancers tweak their nipples, only leer while they writhe on small stages jammed tight between our legs. We claim victory by blowing desperate breath on indifferent pussies, but although they spread themselves open to our appetites, these women defy our hunger.

But let's not fit them for glass slippers just yet. Strippers aren't noble victims. They are low; it's just that we are lower.

They are our fantasies. We are no one's. We pay good money — earned as cops and teachers and workers jangling on the end of jackhammers — to watch these bodies bend. Our monkey brains do handsprings to memorize each peak and valley on every female landscape so that later, in painful privacy, we can dredge each one from the sludge and fuck them all.

But back home masturbation takes too long, partly because I'm drunk but also because I can't remember the individual women. Just a clutter of sculpted mannequin parts that belong to something aloof and unknowable. Something too far removed from my tribal tree to serve me in this degrading time of need. Give me the scars, the smell of her sweat, and what she looks like when she's sad and tired and sick of eating the world's shit sandwiches.

My fantasy begins with a cavalcade of perfect anonymous body parts, but inevitably ends with the lumpy-arsed redhead from two doors down. The one who smokes her Players to the filter and lets her Doberman shit wherever. I take her from behind, slapping her ass, and I come soundlessly to the dying animal noises I imagine she makes with her nasal voice.

And then I'm done. Another lonely night squashed dead-dog flat. As I lie panting, dancers emerge from the club and head home. Some go to empty apartments, some to children, some to loser pimps and drunks and crackheads, and some to understanding men with clear eyes and welcoming hearts. But on some instinctive level — like knowing I'm hungry or have to piss — I understand that none of these women will go home to someone like me.

Draping my leg over the pillow, I hug it in tight. It smells like me. Me alone.

Swimming with Grace

As I see it, there are lots of different people in the world. Big people, small people, white people, brown people, bald-headed people, long-haired people, calm people and people with quarter-inch fuses like my old man. You've got your singers and dancers and yodellers and rock-and-roll guitar boys alongside your poets and pilots and pediatricians.

Despite this wide array, many people can be categorized in a single instant, or after a simple exchange of words. Oops, he's a materialistic sap. She's a drama queen. He's a small "l" liberal. She's a racist bitch. He's a frizzy-haired radical with no real sense of politics beyond the gun-powder whiff of revolution. She's a clown. He's a fruit. She's a nut, but a nut with nice tits, etc. etc.

Once you find the pigeonhole in which to slot them you can just settle back and nod and answer accordingly. "Uh-huh, that really is a swell new sports car, chum. You must be very proud." Face it, most people — and I put myself near the top of this list — aren't worth expending the energy and imagination of real conversation or confrontation. Better just to dismiss them with tongue in cheek and a condescending pat on the rump and send them skipping along on their dim-witted way.

See, ninety-nine percent of the world starts out in the shallow end of this cosmic petri dish. The ambitious few who decide to dog-paddle for deeper waters soon find themselves in over their head. They drown stupidly, clutching for the liquid surface and taking in water with gaping mouths. It's Nature's way of making sure that the idiots never mingle with the special people floating way out there on their backs and indulging in great meditations on the parabolic journey of the sun and the infinite blueness of the sky.

But I once knew a woman (I could never really call her my woman) who was different. She, too, was a special one who, I suspect, must have been born in the deepest part of the dish where the tides run cool and clear.

This woman was different because the first time I laid eyes on her, she was swimming her way methodically toward us splashers in the shallow end. Unlike those other gifted people who were content to bob around in the insular confines of deep water and deeper thought, she wanted to sample everything — even the murk where me and my buffoonish ilk sloshed about. She was the goddess who traipsed down from Olympus.

The problem is, when you make that break you tend to piss off Zeus and Poseidon and Jesus and Vishnu and Athena and Thor and Buddha and Achilles and Allah and even that big bastard on the fringe, Hercules.

I was standing there in my regular little waist-deep patch of water yukking it up with the other imbeciles when I spotted her churning over the horizon. I stopped in mid-yuk, jaw swinging like an unlatched gate.

She was heading straight for us and it made me giddy. It made us all giddy. We weren't used to seeing anyone coming toward us like that. We huddled together and hooted, pooling our excitement, awe and fear. One by one, members of our superstitious little pod peeked out at that beautiful, daring swimmer. Some mumbled rote prayers while others, like myself, forgot the words altogether.

The Gods were furious. The harder she swam and the closer she got to being able to finally plant her lovely kicking feet on the sandy bottom, the more lightning bolts those omnipotent motherfuckers chucked at her. They didn't want her to rest. Didn't want her to stand among the morons and risk letting them become enchanted by her magic. I guess they thought it would spoil us forever. It sure as shit spoiled the fuck out of me.

Huge whitecaps crashed down on her and tried to drive her to the bottom. Spinning water devils darted around her and spit brine in her eyes and knife-edged shoals bit at her legs and ribs and hands. But she kept swimming and swimming and swimming and swimming. Through the rip tides and over the undertows, her shoulders rolled like good poetry was meant to do.

But brilliance, strength and courage all have their limits. Shit, every now and then even Zeus has to kick up his feet and let the world just run itself. I could see she was tiring. Her arms were heavy and she was running low in the water. "Bastards," I thought, but none too loud lest the Gods hurl a spare thunderbolt into my earhole. I instinctively edged out toward her. For the first time in my life I felt the water close in around my throat. My gang hugged one and other, barred their teeth and screeched doomsday warnings. "Keep swimming, woman," I prayed.

Waves, whirlpools and wind stood between her and rest. Maybe she could have made it on her own, we'll never know. With one tentative step I found myself without any footing. I started to stroke like I had seen her do. My feet waved helplessly in the hungry blue abyss.

Looking down I could see the ghostly forms of those intrepid louts who had cast off before me. Big bulging eyes, and swollen tongues being nibbled away by crabs. Bumbling Galileos who charted courses straight to ocean's bottom, claiming useless, shifting sandbars in the name of impetuous simple-mindedness. I swam harder.

Oh fuck, it was tough going for a simpleton like me. The trouble with swimming is that it isn't just a question of swimming. It involves thinking and finding a rhythm and choosing the right bearing and locating that part of your soul where the impetus to swim originates. I had spent the better part of my days just wading around drinking, eating, pissing and sunburning my shoulders. Now my muscles ached, my head throbbed, my heart pumped. For the first time I was alive enough to be afraid of dying.

And suddenly — bang! — our heads collided. She looked at me with wide-eyed surprise and an exhausted smile. I fell in love and coughed a mouthful of seawater in her face. Then I wrapped her tired arms around my neck and started that long voyage home.

I heard an angry howl bang down from up high. By now the Gods were really trying to fuck us over. It was bad enough that one of their own had turned her back on the sacred clique, but now one of the single-cell peons had jumped into the fray. This was more than just a mutiny, it was a revolution. Thousands of miles away, in a dingy basement, that same frizzy-haired radical cried, "Fuck the establishment" from behind a stack of pamphlets. Right on, dude. Keep packing that TNT.

The Gods had rolled up their sleeves and were getting ready to go to town on my mortal head. If I had been smart enough to remember the lessons of Prometheus and Sisyphus, I may have just let her sink right there. Luckily I was armed with that special kind of shortsighted bravery found only in the very dumb and the very smitten. I just kept windmilling my arms, trying to catch the occasional breaker and keeping my sights on shore. She lay her head between my shoulders and I'm betting she shut her eyes and sighed. Rest.

The problem was that I was a wader, not a swimmer. I had already burned off the bulk of my energy thrashing my way out to meet her. We were a long way from home and the Gods were really looking to scuttle us. A man can only go so far fueled on beer and new love. I started fading. Fast. I was taking on water like a rotten schooner. Each mouthful of salt weighed a ton in my belly and the pull to the bottom was magnetic. I was going under.

Then I felt her arms tighten around my chest. Her warm, liquid mouth pressed down on my neck and, just like that, I was the strongest man in the world. I was Mark fucking Spitz. But I didn't need the gaggle of gold medals hanging around my neck. All I needed was her. I butterflied and crawled and porpoise-kicked my way through the rollers like the goddamned hero I never was. I used my broad body like a surfboard and we rode the lip curls of waves. She laughed in my ear and let out a whoop and I screamed, "Fuck yes," in absolute animal glee.

Then it all stopped. Wind and rain and torrential down-pours — they just tucked their tails between their legs and chicken-shitted it back home. The Gods knew they were whipped. Every now and then — not very often, mind you — the stars line up just right and your tea leaves settle just so and you turn up just the Tarot card you were looking for and — *bango!* — even you can beat the Gods and their stacked, stinking odds.

She slipped off my back and dove deep beneath the calm surface, sweet ass grinning up at the sun. I did the same. Even under water her smile was hot and it steamed like good

Club Love

Last month, I picked up a woman in a favourite haunt of mine; a place called, ridiculously enough, Club Love. Jane was a battered old barfly disguised as a waitress but, to her credit, she was still putting up a scrap.

There was no artistry in Jane's heavy makeup or Jell-O mould hair. Nothing beautiful about the pudding ass she jiggled in front of the boys and me every night. Nevertheless, that gin-lacquered artifact put a knot in my chinos just for answering the bell every night. It's the strange erotic charge I get watching the unwinnable struggle against decay and decrepitude. Hemingway can have the blatant gush and roar of the bullfights, I'll take Venice and its slow descent into the sea.

Back in the 70s, Club Love was a good bar, one of the prime spots in town. All the men wore dark suits and took long, confident strides across the tile, hooked at the elbows with leggy women dangling spangles and pearls. People laughed and got liquored, but no one ever went stupid. No glasses were ever smashed, no punches ever thrown. It was the kind of place that made you feel good about stopping in for a drink, the kind of place that gave you hope that you might just be making it after all.

But in the 80s, Club Love became a biker bar, and the Italian suits and manicures gave way to biceps and bandanas. At first, the regulars tried to stand their ground, tried to cling to their little Xanadu by bucking bellies with the bearded invaders. But eyes that scan quarterly reports have no chance in a stare down. Not against the beasts. An ass grab of a matron of the arts, a tense exchange of words and a mangled nose for a claims adjuster was all it took to stampede the dress pants back uptown, cuff-links and squash rackets in tow. Cops carted off a few of the red-asses, but the turf war was over before it really began. I don't care how cutthroat they claim business is; no man ever grew real balls sitting in a boardroom.

The big hairy boys settled in for a good long stay and Club Love changed forever. I kept going because I lived right next door and I've always been a lazy drunk. Just traded in my shiny shoes and pick-up patter for construction boots and silence. I kept my same spot at the bar, paid my tab regularly and never made eye contact with the mouth-breathers who swaggered by sporting tattooed faces. The bikers didn't pay me no mind, didn't hassle me. To them I might as well have been a chair that drank too much rye.

But a high-profile biker war tested our mayor's patience, especially after an innocent old crossing guard named Eunice McCaffrey was gunned down in the crossfire. The public howled for justice. An elite anti-gang squad was formed and the cops began leaning on everyone wearing colours.

For two months an unmarked van was parked right in front of Club Love and you could all but hear the clicking of cameras whenever a Harley rumbled up. A series of city-wide raids turned up caches of drugs and weapons and a stable of runaway farm girls enslaved as whores. Every day the papers trumpeted new arrests and carried shots of scowling outlaws being hauled into the courthouse clad in denim and handcuffs.

Generally, bikers get a kick out of publicity — one wall in the bar was papered with news clippings of their nasty handiwork. But this time the glare was too much, even for them. They started whispering hard into each other's earholes while they drank and it was plain to see that they were getting spooked.

Before then, the boys from Club Love had had precious few pretenders looking to challenge them for their throne. Their litany of brutal slayings put the shrink on even the biggest pair of stones, and the other gangs decided that it was safer to hang out on the periphery waiting for a stumble than to risk a frontal assault. Sometimes a biker's greatest weapon is patience.

In that racket, rivals smell weakness like a shark sniffs out a swimmer with a gaping leg wound. When Club Lovers started getting scooped up and jailed in the police dragnets, the others saw it as an opening. Almost overnight, authorities started fishing dead Club Lovers out of the river, chained up in sleeping bags and weighed down with cinder blocks. Tossed off of bridges in the middle of the night like pillowcases full of murderous kittens.

No music was playing when I walked into the bar the day after Coco and Little John were dredged up, bellies bloated with bad water. All you could hear was the sound of creaking leather and hard breathing. I turned on my heel and left. No matter what the experts say, sometimes drinking alone is *absolutely* the best thing a man can do for his health.

Having to square off against cops and other gangs at the same time was too much, especially out in the open like that. Might as well have painted great big bulls' eyes on their backs. The boys from Club Love must've got the bug-out directive from someone in the upper echelon because one day they all straddled their bikes and rolled away for good. Run out of Dodge, they set up shop in big concrete bunkers built on private land way out of town where they could barricade themselves in for a spell and regroup.

Club Love never recovered. For better or worse, it had been one of the city's most famous spots for twenty years. But its new owners didn't give a shit. The good clubs take aim at a certain clientele and lure them in. You run a bar for businessmen or bikers or neighbourhood guys looking to quench their thirst after another day wearing the blue collar yoke, whatever. But these monkeys had no plan, unless cornering the market on dank qualified as a plan.

They changed nothing and fixed nothing and by the mid-90s Club Love still wore yellowed news stories about bikers named Billy Shakespeare and Short Leg and The Chinaman. And when you took a piss you still eyeballed such pithy biker truisms as *Keep 'em shiny side up and rolling straight* and *There is no justice. Just us.*

The one thing Club Love did have was Jane. She was a holdover from the biker years; a tall, wild blonde with Janice Joplin glasses who had first rode in with her arms putting the squeeze around some brute called The Spoiler. Jane really loved that guy and, for a mangler, he seemed all right — so long as he was with her. Sometimes the two of them sat at the bar away from the War Table where the other gorillas sprawled and farted, and I'd hear them talking about regular people stuff like houses and kids.

But it always seemed like The Spoiler was reeled back in just when he was ready to make some sort of significant break.

He was Red Louie's right-hand man, known both for his ability to negotiate the tricky deals and for his proficiency with a sawed-off when negotiations fell through. According to what I heard around me, when The Spoiler saw blood he turned into a regular Berserker. One legend has it that immediately following the infamous Monday Massacre shootout with the Killjoys he calmly walked around the battlefield, pissing into the bodies of his still alive, but mortally wounded, rivals.

I can't say I ever saw that side of The Spoiler. He was relatively quiet for that bunch, spending most of his time at Club Love drinking quarts of beer and making Jane laugh. As far as I could see, he treated her well, better than many of the Gino Cappuccinos used to treat their showcase women. He was attentive and strangely gallant, pouring beer for her and rubbing the back of her neck. And whenever one of the boys, even Big Louie, tried to interrupt his conversation with Jane, The Spoiler would shut them up by holding one big finger up in the air, never taking his eyes off of his woman until she was done.

It was easy to see why Jane got the special treatment though. When she was young, she was a real piece of work, proof positive that God's handiwork is all around us, even here on the basement level of this cosmic totem pole. Back then, there was something about the way she walked into a room that made a man cough up his love, even those of us who kept that dangerous shit under lock and key. She wasn't outrageously beautiful, but she had a smile that looked like she was in cahoots with Life, like she had it all figured out.

Unlike lots of the biker broads, Jane didn't take their shit without a fight. She was fearless. I saw her turn Goose into a screaming heap with a knee to the 'nads after he pawed at one of her big tits without asking first. She was the only woman who the bikers respected and treated almost as an equal. They sought her out and asked her advice when things weren't rolling their way. A cross between Calamity Jane and Ann Landers.

But when the whole mob of them blew out of town Jane hung back and took a job at the bar. I don't know why she didn't follow. It didn't help that her and The Spoiler had had a major falling out and that he had started throwing it into some teenage tramp, even though he still looked at Jane from his seat at the War Table with the saddest eyes you'll ever see on a killer. Maybe she was just lazy like me or maybe she had had enough of getting to know young men just in time to watch them die. I'm guessing she was just looking to lay low and fig- ured you couldn't get any lower than Club Love.

And so Jane and I stayed put, me clinging to my chair at the bar while she started waiting tables. She was too smart to keep paying for booze in a shit hole like that, better to get paid and drink for free. Me? I might as well have been cutting rent checks.

But all those years at the bar didn't do either of us any favours, and both of us became caricatures of people who had spent too many nights stuck to the skinny end of the bottle. Yeah, surprise, surprise. We both got old before we were ready, both slapped on extra weight — her on her arms and thighs and me on a thick rind suffocating my waist. A bar'll do that to you if you don't take heed; turn the hard, sharp edges of youth into a mound, soft and bloodshot.

Over the years, Jane and I got friendly. You can't spend that much time sitting just three feet from a person and not start yakking. Nothing big, nothing personal, mind you, just that soulless bar banter that people toss around to kill the gaps between pulls of beer.

Jane and I hooked up with a new Club Love crew, a bunch of hard-drinking boys from the docks. These were decent fellows who earned good money with their backs and legs and weren't afraid to spend it. They liked me because I could make them laugh and they liked Jane because she took their bullshit without flinching. "Jesus H. Christ, Jane," Charley once laughed, "how'd you get so bullet-proof?" They didn't know about Jane's long run with the bikers, didn't know about her learning triage on the fly, didn't know how the very bar on which they tossed their peanut shells had soaked up its share of her tears.

She looked at me with a small, surprised, smile — happy that I had never spilled the beans to them on a night when she wasn't working. Hers is exactly the kind of tale that bar gossips trade like currency. But what the fuck, I've never made it my business to yak about someone else's. It was her life to live, her story to tell. I raised my glass in an imperceptible toast that only the two of us drank to.

By midnight the boys had cleared out and it was just Jane and I up at the bar, her on one side and me on the other. I was getting sauced and was flirting pretty heavy, keeping a close eye on her big jugs. A goddamned photo finish in a zeppelin race. She kept pulling on a cigarette, those long magical hauls of people who've been smoking since age eight but who'll never die of cancer or emphysema or black lung or any of that terrifying shit. Big, mighty drags that flamed the tip and topped off her miraculous lungs with great wafts of smoke and stale bar smells.

Sweet Christ! With every never-ending draw her fun bags shimmied like a broken-down oasis in whose waters, I suspected, a man could still slake a thirst.

"McVie," she laughed. "You're staring at my tits again."

"Yes. Indeed I am," I said. She laughed again. Bingo, I was in.

She took me to her small apartment. It was neat, but cramped with cats and the kind of mismatched furniture your parents give you when you first move out. In the middle of a low coffee table there was a framed photo of her and The Spoiler zooming down a stretch of highway laughing and in love, both of their manes flying straight back and free. I've never been on a motorcycle, never had long hair, never felt very free. But the plus side of that equation is that I don't often fall in love and I rarely have to piece together my heart when relationships slick out on a oily curve. My apartment is near empty and I don't hang on to photographs. I don't hang on to much.

At my request she poured us a couple of fingers of rye. It wasn't very good, but then again, rye rarely is. We talked a long time, too long for my liking. She confessed that her and Mike, which turned out to be The Spoiler's real name, used to play a guessing game in which they would speculate who the hell I was in life. "I always bet that you were just another waste case, another lost soul," she said with a hard grin. "But Mike liked to say that you were a poet from Argentina or an old boxing champ or a bank robber on the run. He liked thinking that people were better than him."

She looked at me for a long, long while and didn't say another word. Funny how life can work like that, all these years sitting in the same bar and she didn't know anything about me. I had her all sized up the second I laid eyes on her. I held her stare and drained my glass.

"You win," I said and led her to the bedroom.

+ + + +

Afterward, we lay doused in sex and she started talking to me like I was someone else, someone who really cared for her. Sex'll do that to some people, open them up like an oyster on the half-shell. She started rambling about her childhood and her pa. How he spent his life blowing up the earth in an east coast gypsum mine. How he got paid good wages, but how he was a nasty piece of New Brunswick. How, when he got on the booze, which was often, he would berate her ma for letting herself get fat and frumpy.

One night Jane woke up with his dirty miner's hand on her twelve-year-old tit. She pushed him away and he smacked her mean and hard across the face. Furious, he climbed on top, hiked up her nightgown and took what she wouldn't give, like tearing gypsum from stubborn rock. He was drunk so it took a long time and she wanted to holler for her ma but shame and guilt had bit out her tongue.

She lay on her back, crying softly. I guess I hadn't sized her up so good after all. Maybe twenty years ago Jane had it all figured out, when the meanest man alive loved her sweetly and she was brim-full of cockiness. But since then Life had been kicking the piss and vinegar out of her, drop by bitter drop.

I was at a loss for what to do. Maybe The Spoiler could have growled the soft words she needed to hear to make her stop crying, to make her feel whole. But not me. I've always been mute in the face of another person's pain. And I didn't have a Harley that we could fly away on so the wind would blow all those ghosts out of her head. No, I didn't have the big tattooed arms to wrap around her and, quite frankly, I didn't want them. I was just a sucker from Club Love looking to fill one night with something other than loneliness. But I had stumbled onto something else, something big and brutal. And now the both of us lay there, trapped.

I looked at Jane from the corner of my eye. Her breasts were flat, like someone had poked them with a pin and deflated all the desire and delight right out of them. Two dead dogs on a lonely stretch of road. Made me think of the photo I saw last summer of two soaking wet sleeping bags being hauled out of the river by grim-faced cops. The caption said that one held the body of Billy Shakespeare, The Spoiler curled dead in the other. It had taken them a while, but the Killjoys finally got their revenge.

I wanted to bolt, wanted to get outside where I could breathe again, but I was cornered. Instead, I shut my eyes and tried not to let Jane's sobs get inside me. Across the ocean, Venice slipped another notch into the dirty, unfeeling water that would, one day, swallow it whole.

Other Stories

Putty in the Locks

When my mother swims she hardly ripples the water, hardly inspires a splash. You've never seen anyone move so slow — you and I could easily slam down three strokes to her one. Thrashers like us would splinter the surface that she barely wrinkles. On calm days mom looks like she's sliding across the top of a mirror, dipping into her own reflection for impetus. If you saw her, your first reaction would be to wonder how she stays afloat at all. But she does. Mile after mile, hour after hour, lake after lake.

I don't really know how she got so proficient in the water. She grew up mostly in the Prairies, Winnipeg, Red Deer and Regina. Most probably on Lake Winnipeg, ringed by its shifting white dunes and stubborn scrub brush. When I was a kid, mom took me and my squirrelly brother Jay to Winnipeg to visit my burly, free-range cousins. My most lasting impression was of the day we spent at the lake, so big you couldn't even see the other side, and so pan-flat that even a short-leg like me could walk for miles before I was in over my head. Jay has an attention deficit disorder and, when he was young, the only things that seemed to grab him for more than five minutes were huge bodies of water. The larger and more barren the horizon, the calmer Jay became, as if uniform endlessness stripped away the anxiety of choice.

Mom was born in Winnipeg and her mother, my grandma, went insane there when mom was very young. I'm not sure, but I think grandma first flipped sometime around mom's ninth birthday. I'm unclear on the details because mom and I hardly ever talk about such matters. We have trouble discussing things like that; things that hurt, things trapped beneath the lake ice, things that tear off a piece of you on their way out. She and I mine from the same fat vein of melancholy, just on opposite sides of the wall.

When I say my grandma went insane I don't mean eccentric crazy, with an army of ugly lawn dwarves and thirteen cats named after members of the Royal Family. Grandma was lock-the-kids-in-a-closet-for-a-whole-day-type crazy. Mom said grandma didn't beat them often, but when she did it was for keeps.

From what I remember about the layout of my grandparents' house from our occasional Christmas visits, there were three upstairs closets, one in which to lock each kid. I remember this because for a period during my childhood I was preoccupied with hiding in closets and tucking myself into crawl spaces. I'd roll myself up in a tight chrysalis of blankets and lie under my bed for hours. Not because I was unhappy or mistreated; I was just drawn to the comforting cocoon of darkness and claustrophobia. Unlike Jay, I needed my world in nice and close. Wide open spaces made me nervous.

I spent one afternoon in the closet in my mom's old room, perched high on a shelf and tinkling the bent wire hangers like chimes. The sound of the grown-ups' voices filtered up through the plaster and floorboards to warm me like furnace heat. No recognizable words, just the soothing murmur and buzz of people who didn't even know I was there among them.

Prior to grandma's illness, their family was the picture of happiness. At least, that is what mom tells me when both of us are up to talking about it. Of course, memories can become romaticized over time and doubly distorted when viewed against the backdrop of the tragedy that swooped in on them like a prairie fire. They do look happy in photos, though. Happy and beautiful, five of them linked at the elbows, striding down Winnipeg's black and white sidewalks in camel hair coats and smiles that you only see in old movies.

It's hard to tell how a person is feeling while they are swimming because their face is mostly underwater. I have always suspected mom is most at peace when she swims, after all, she does it every day. Then again, I do lots of things daily that don't make me happy, like peeling myself away from a warm body in my bed and shaving and squeezing onto the bus and dragging myself to work.

Mom makes us laugh when she tells us about the turf wars being waged at the YMCA every morning during the Senior Early Bird Swim. She claims that many of the regulars will kick at you if you try and pass them. I ask her if she ever unsheathes her infamously snaggled "razor toe" when the going gets rough. She takes a long haul on a du Maurier and deadpans, "Oh, there's blood in the water, all right." For Christmas I bought her Speedo goggles with lightning bolt holographs that flash across the eyes. My brother has taken to calling her Sharky.

Mom had a whack of uncles and aunts around her when she was growing up, but no one ever mentioned The Madness. For 50 more years, not a word. That side of the clan is long dead, many members snuffed out through tragedies of their own or having dragged ill fortune into the grave behind them like a bloody, telltale corpse. Although I hardly remember them, their blighted history makes me think of the Kennedys — only without the political power and Hyannisport compound.

I have this lasting impression of their big, grain-fed family sitting around the massive wooden table at Uncle Westy's farm, laughing and joking and carrying on at the top of their lungs. Doing everything but addressing grandma's insanity, trying to drown out the pain and suffering with the boisterous ring of prairie togetherness. Strong arms wrapped around each other's shoulders, swaying and belting out "Roll Out the Barrel," but never once whispering counsel to my mom or the two boys.

Yes, everyone on that side of the family is dead, but their thunderous silence is alive and well, coursing through my mother's body like an infection. Something chronic but not terminal.

Even rare talks with my mother on this subject are buffeted by silence, punched full of soundless bullet holes. Large chunks of history are omitted or locked away in her air-tight emotional vault. I don't know if she has such terrible difficulty talking to me about it because of my own discomfort in hearing it, or vice versa. I do not ask many questions and, while I nod sympathetically, I am unable to make eye contact. In many ways I am still the little boy who seeks comfort in the dark. Some things should never see light.

She once told me that the doctors wanted to incarcerate grandma indefinitely, but that gramps couldn't bear it.

Couldn't bear the thought of his storybook wife grinding teeth marks deep into the hard rubber paddles that orderlies jammed in her mouth whenever the doctors tried to set her straight with electric shocks. Like my mom, grandma was sharp and had a dry wit and once told my father with a lucid smile that "growing old isn't for sissies."

So gramps took her home, on two separate occasions, even though she made his life hell. Even though she'd lock her kids in closets for whole days. Even though she had clearly become a monster.

Gramps was a remarkably noble man, my mom's hero. We grandkids loved him too because he was big and smoked "ceegars" and told us homemade stories about improbable heroes called Hammertoe Joe and Barry Barrel Gut. He insisted that his middle names included Cicero, Falstaff, Balthazar, Hercules and Fauntleroy.

During one of his last visits to Montreal he broke his toe playing football with us but he didn't stop punting. He joined our secret boys' club in the basement, called the Robin Hood and His Merry Men Club, and even mailed us a $5 initiation fee. My mother saves the letter in her night table drawer and we all take it out from time to time and read it. It is very formal and very funny, written by a man who understood that children running clubs in basements relish both.

Gramps could have left grandma locked away and no one would have blamed him. Could have paid her visits and taken her out for monthly walks and remarried and have been happy and no one would have looked askew. But he didn't, because (I think my mom told me) he could never forget who grandma was before, when she was beautiful and brilliant and the sun around which the whole family twirled.

But his choice affected his children. I don't know my uncles very well, so I can't speak for them. But my mom carries pain and bitterness in her all the time. She grew to hate her mother, not so much because of what grandma did to her, but what she did to gramps. She told me that the kids kept the abuse amongst themselves so as not to add another burden to gramps' load, afraid that it would drive him mad too.

They never told gramps how she'd charge at them with her eyes flashing, screaming obscenities. Never told him how she'd drag them to the closets by the hair —mom, the oldest, first, then Uncle Mike and, lastly, Baby Petey.

Mostly, grandma would lock them up and storm downstairs to clean and cook and wash at a maniacal pace. Gramps never knew that the house looked its best when his children were suffering most. Sometimes, however, grandma would stand outside each closet and slide in whispered poison about what evil children they were — like pouring biting red fire ants under the door. But mom says the most terrifying times were when she could hear grandma on the other side, saying nothing, just breathing hard like a beast in a zoo.

No, they never told gramps. Instead, mom kissed away her brothers' tears and willed away her own. She turned each closet into a giant treasure chest, hiding things like flashlights and candies and colouring books and small wooden tops for her brothers to find once they had stopped wailing. The boys were coached on how to recognize the creaking third step on the staircase and squirrel away the toys before grandma threw open the door and released them from their wooden cell.

But grandma claimed gramps' life as her own, tainting it with her illness. She would berate him and hit him and make the most horrific accusations, but only in private. In public she was sweet and matronly, like she had just hopped off a Rockwell canvas.

Decade after decade, gramps served as her caretaker and shouldered her mad hatred for him like a cross. But I never saw him sad. He was always so generous with his hugs and laughter, and I remember wishing there weren't so many miles of train track lying between Montreal and Winnipeg.

One day, long after the children had grown up and married, gramps came home after work and found grandma on the floor, unconscious. She had overdosed on pills. Suicide. He called the ambulance and they saved her, rewarding him with another fifteen years of her despotic reign. The doctor told him how, if he had come home a few minutes later, she would have died. My mother told me — and this I *do* remember like a horse remembers a branding iron — how every day she lives with the guilt of wishing gramps had been caught in traffic.

Sometimes my mother drinks and spits venom at us. I try not to let it sting, telling myself it is just grandma talking from the grave.

Once mom admitted that she lives every day with the fear that grandma's madness may, one day, be her own. Or worse yet, her children's. I have no answer for that, no words of comfort, because, I too fear the same. It took me 30 years to understand why mom had dad plug all the closet locks with putty when we first moved into our house.

That is why I wish you could see her swim. Well into her 60s, mom can still go and go, and even though it seems like she is hardly making any headway, there is a fearlessness in the face of distance and depth that belies her timid nature. When she strokes with her left arm, the side on which she takes her breath, it rotates so long and so slowly it makes you think of the inexorable journey of the sun. Makes you think of eternity.

Once, when I was a young teenager on the verge of becoming a world-class athlete, I challenged her to swim across Lake

Memphremagog. I took off like a young Tarzan, but when I neared the centre my strength started slipping away. Every time I took a stroke it seemed like I couldn't get enough air into my lungs. I tried to force myself onward, tried not to think about how cold the water gets out in the middle, tried not to imagine the monsters lurking down below past the algae and silt.

But I had started too fast, too full of the papier-mâché courage that comes with youth. I burned out like a Roman candle and my sudden weakness scared me. It flooded my headstrong and confident reservoirs with terror and insecurity. Unable to find the strength, inner or otherwise, I was pulled blue and sputtering into the rowboat by the armpits.

On the way back in, the boat carrying me passed mom. She was barely moving but still inching forward. I watched the rest of her swim from the dock, wrapped in big beach towels. Onlookers charted her progress with binoculars and asked me if I wanted to look. I refused, not because I was angry at being beaten by my housewife mother, I just found great comfort in watching her so small and brave on the horizon. She made it across and became my hero that day.

Swimming gives us all a glimpse of her resolve that often goes overlooked. We are a family defined by strength, a collection of boxers and weightlifters and rugby players, and it takes a loud voice and sharp elbows to carve out your niche at our table.

However, when we finally had to put down our beloved dog Babe, dad, my brother and I fell to pieces at the vet's. Mom was the rock. While the rest of us sobbed and paced around death's periphery as the injection was taking hold and stopping Babe's heart, mom was down on the floor, pressing up against her dog's soft muzzle and whispering what a beautiful, brave girl she was. I'll never forget the image of my mom kneeling in the large pool of urine that seeped from Babe's corpse, still pouring soothing words into ears that no longer could hear.

A few summers ago mom and dad rented a cottage in Alburg, Vermont, just over the border and perched above Lake Champlain. I cycled down from Montreal, another phony test of strength and endurance that I periodically subject myself to that really has nothing to do with either.

When I arrived I was hot and exhausted and my mother was waiting for me with a sandwich and a cold Molson Ex. I wolfed down the tuna and wandered down to the side of the lake to enjoy my beer. Dad was bare-chested on the balcony reading the paper. The day was perfect and sunny, and the thin spun-candy clouds dissolved on the lips of the wind. Mom walked down the short hill, snapping her bathing cap over her ears, smiling at me.

No longer is she the sparrow-boned Winnipeg girl who looked like Audrey Hepburn in photographs. The girl who travelled across Europe and fell in love with a vacationing Iranian prince. The girl who, my father likes to joke, won his heart on their first date because she ordered her beer by the quart.

Now she is broad and strong across the shoulders and hips, a woman who has carried the burden of guilt and love and responsibility for most of her life. A woman who, by default, was the sister, daughter, wife and mother in a household of men. She has grown powerful and thick from clasping three of her own children to her breasts and nourishing them with her body. A woman who accepted the sheer weight of sadness and silence but refused to let it crush her. Hers is a body made strong by survival.

She walks gingerly through the shallows because for the first fifteen feet the bottom is a razored obstacle course of freshwater clams. But once clear of the shells, she strides through the water, slowly cupping handfuls over her shoulders and arms. Her eyes are fixed straight ahead.

And then she pushes off toward the opposite shore, casting herself into the water like baptism. Her feet hardly kick, raising no splash at all. My mom has gone through life without making a single wave. Shoulders roll slowly in their sockets, a stroke made smooth and precise by repetition. Her white skin stands out on the dark blue water. She is alone.

I take a long pull of beer and the carbonated burn feels good in my throat. Squinting into the afternoon sun, I remember feeling alone on Memphremagog even though my friends were bobbing beside me in the boat. I remember how frightened I became peering down into the depths where there was no bottom. My heart beat fast and fearful in that vast endless place and I wished I were somewhere else, somewhere small and finite. A closet.

Sitting on that Vermont shore I wonder what my mother felt as a child locked away from the world, barred from sunlight and the companionship of friends. I wonder where she got the strength to keep going, the strength to feel love and hate and guilt all at the same time. I wonder how she was able to rise from those ashes and bless us all with her example. More than anything I wonder why mom, once she set foot on the distant shore, ever chose to turn around and come home.

Watching her in the water, I am amazed at her grace and strength. Yes, you might wonder how she stays afloat at all, but I know mom can swim forever.

The Critical Moment

So we've just had sex pretty good sex you know 'cause it's Saturday afternoon and I'm always at my best on weekends after lunch when I'm fat on sleep and feel-good food and feel-better beer and as far away from the gnaw of punch cards and back taxes as I can possibly get in the 48 angel-winged hours that separate Glorious Friday from Craphole Monday and I'm lying on my back looking for hidden pictures in the stucco ceiling and she's draped across me like warm linen and I'm thinking how I've got it going pretty good for a guy with high school and a beer gut but then I notice that she's crying and I ask What's Wrong 'cause now I'm worried that I might have called her the wrong name at a climactic juncture or maybe I bruised a tender spot poking around with my awkward thumb but she gives me one of those crumbly chin-trembler smiles and says I'm Not Crying 'Cause I'm Sad I'm 'Crying Cause I'm So Very Happy

So then it's my turn to whip off a cheese-eating smile of my own and I say That's Great Baby but in my head I'm screaming Run You Stupid Sonofabitch Run 'cause my experience with women has taught me that when they start crying out of happiness is exactly the same moment they've lined you up dead in the crosshairs of their Long-Range Rifle and that the phrase

So Very Happy really means *This Will Be A Difficult Relationship From Which To Extricate Yourself* or *I'm Giving You A Head Start Before I Begin Shooting*

So right then and there I decide that I won't be seeing her any more after today but the thought fucks me up more than a bit 'cause she's pressing her cheek against my chest and I'm pouring my heartbeat into her ear and she's stroking my sticky dick like a james bond villain on a white persian cat while her hot tears of happiness are splashing off my ribs like french spring water and I may be a self-serving prick but I'm just not one of those guys who can cut loose a decent woman with a snap of his fingers and feel smug about it

And to tell you the truth I'm more than a little surprised by this whole weepy turn of events 'cause I've been assuming all along that she was just in it for the mindless bouncy fun like me especially since I had gone out of my way to be both a particularly good ride and such a dull conversationalist that no woman would ever want to hang anything on my skin peg for more than a rousing afternoon or a long holiday weekend tops

But you know how the mind works and in the space of a few seconds I speed read through page after page of my pathetic twenty-volume relationship history and I realize how this certainly isn't the first time I've been blindsided by a woman and jesus christ when it comes to reading women I'm a goddamned hillbilly illiterate and I smile at my little joke which isn't good 'cause she catches me happy-facing and drops her cheek into the sanctuary of my collarbone and squeezes my knob a bit and fires off a few more teardrops and I can feel it running through her skinny arms like voltage that she believes my smile was in honour of her So Very Happy-ness when it most surely wasn't and it is plain as plain can be that at this exact space in time I have reached *The Critical Moment*

When I have to make things perfectly clear 'cause it is essential that we slaughter this newborn thing of hers before its shaky legs start getting stronger underneath itself and it bolts free across the savanna but I can't come right out and tell her any of this 'cause as I mentioned before our previous conversations have been so uniformly insipid that we are entirely without precedent when it comes to initiating a serious exchange of ideas

But she's looking up at me with wet eyes and I do what all men naturally do when we are faced with a crying woman which is to panic and tack a wooden smile across my wordless mouth in desperate hope that that will be good enough but I remember how she is especially receptive to smiles at this moment so I wipe the stupid grin off my face which causes her some concern and I can tell that the next two words out of her mouth will most certainly be What's Wrong and that absolutely is the last issue I want to broach as I am still trying to decide if I want to break up with her later that night over the phone even though I don't want to be premature and get my arse tossed out of paradise just 'cause of a brief moment of stupidity and terror

So before she can pop the What's part of the What's Wrong question out of her mouth I kiss her good and slick on her fat lips 'cause she likes her guys to play He-Man Master of the Universe and her hand tightens around my soft dick and even though I just had a great big happy orgasm a mere ten minutes before and I am certainly no longer a miraculous boy of twenty her squeeze whooshes a handful of primer blood through the spongy chambers of my groggy knob and the engine room starts creaking but just before the motor coughs to life I am nailed between the eyes with the realization that this is the first time I'd ever kissed her without being motivated by anything other than pure lust

Now I've kissed lots of women before for many reasons other than lust including love and happiness and grief and boredom and homelessness and curiosity and sometimes just out of dull habit but never her partially because it was all still fairly new between us and it is par for the course that there is a lot of hormonal yippee juice flowing at that early stage but I had this comforting feeling that it would always be like that with her 'cause she seemed so honestly happy to pull me down onto her mattress time and time and time again and I say honestly happy meaning that she seemed to love the sex for the sex itself and not for all the other extraneous long-term scenarios involving houses and kids and floppy-eared dogs that many post-orgasmic women wrongly attach to a few fun-filled hours of howled horniness

After all just 'cause I happen to know my way around a woman's most intimate parts does not immediately mean I can navigate the precarious minefield of interpersonal relationships with the guarantee that we will both keep our legs and hearts shrapnel-free 'cause if you want me to let you in on a secret I'm shit-scared of women and I'm starting to think that I only got good at sex to avoid talking to them altogether and it's always dumbfounded me how a lot of perfectly sensible women get all ga-ga over good sex not that it shouldn't merit a yee-haw and a joyous click of the heels but I have yet to fall in love with a woman based solely on her merits as a fellationist and I most certainly don't want to sound arrogant but on at least three occasions during particularly successful sex I have seen the actual transition from lust to love float down over a woman's eyes like a gauzy veil through which reality is forever altered and the old movie soft-focus trickery takes away my edges which is ironic 'cause I am of the opinion that it is exactly those edges that make me fun in the sack and I know I'm rambling but all I really want to do is find a woman who won't coronate me as some sort of philosopher king just 'cause I give good head

But this woman just seemed so dreamily horny that I was under the unfortunately wrong impression that she didn't really look much farther down the road than our next bumpity-hump and I am being totally sincere when I say that I really really felt almost blessed for having stumbled upon this remarkable creature because strange as it may sound her unspoken enthusiasm for the fleshy here-and-now had started making me think that she was the kind of woman I could hang with for a very long time

Of course that was before she screwed it up by saying the dreaded So Very Happy words and I fully realize how contradictory this makes me sound and that I come off looking like King Arsehole in a universe of stinkholes for being spooked by three words that in comparison to The Really Big Three (which are of course I Love You) are so damned innocuous that it's laughable but if I am going to be perfectly honest about things I have to say that I have much fewer problems with I Love You than So Very Happy 'cause I am of the mind that compared to real happiness love is much easier to fool ourselves into believing we have found and if a woman cries because she is happy it is only further proof of how difficult a thing it is to find and by extension if I am the source of that tear-inducing happiness it puts an inordinate amount of spine-bending pressure upon my already suspect shoulders

But the kiss is fine and the cock squeeze is even finer and somehow she draws out the guilt I am feeling for having started this sexual preamble just to shut her up and swallows it down to her belly and guts and sex spots and I hover there for a few minutes in between thought and horniness which in turn causes me more concern 'cause I hate mixing the two since it has again been my experience that this is generally the precursor to the end of that carefree honeymoon period in which sex rules the day and anxieties and insecurities and rectal exams and nut-busting floor bosses and creeping diseases of the heart and gums and soul are all shelved in lieu of a huffy-puffy screw and an ass-slapping yodel or two

You see thought is like a vampire 'cause once it has been invited across the threshold it loiters in your bedside shadows looking for a free meal on an exposed vein or artery and the second it sinks its hollowed fangs into your fleshy fun is the same moment that your sexual sanctuary is forever tainted by outside worries and stresses and if that's the case I generally find it more satisfying to whack myself off into oblivion just before I go to sleep so that I can pass out before the blood-sucking thinking demons swoop down from the rafters 'cause no matter how highly we regard wisdom and education and all its cerebral trappings thought is what slaughters our animal joy and stands as the great dental dam between us and the sweet salty juices that make up a good life and make up a good night and make up a good world worth repopulating with other like-bodied beasts

Didn't eve's poisoned gift get us the bum's rush out of eden and didn't it come in the form of a candied apple pill tweaked from the tree of knowledge and isn't god's final message just this Hey Assholes Leave The Thinking To Me You Just Concentrate On Getting Laid but eve couldn't leave good enough alone and now we're sentenced to spend our every waking moment chafing in ties and pinching leather shoes and double breasted yokes while we try to get women drunk enough at night so we can connive and coerce them back into that original state of nakedness and grace which was once our every day

But sweet christ her mouth has some sort of magic power over me doesn't it and while I grapple with these higher issues my intentions slip wonderfully crotchward and quick as slick shit out my alimentary canal I am lying on my back gazing up at her fat round titties bouncing around like beautiful twin suns at the centre of my moment's stuccoed universe and I am smiling and pig-grunting and touching her and looking her in the eyes where I see hope and fear and the snap crackle pop of potential happiness and I would be lying if I said that that potential didn't tug at me 'cause in spite of all my protestations in regards to the elusive nature of happiness I'm as much a sucker for the stuff as the next lonely bastard sitting with his heart and guts crammed up against the bar

But it also pisses me off that she would burden me with her hopes and shackle my spirit to her aspirations and inextricably weave her preconceived notions of partnership and coupledom and familial happiness to my afraid-to-be-anything-but-single ass 'cause I know firsthand that I get worn down by the long haul and that my legs will most certainly falter beneath the deadweight crush of her dreams and the inescapable monotony of the marathoner's tread.

Besides by pinning her hopes on to me so too she promises to dole out daily servings of happiness which is a sweet picture to be sure but a goddamned lie if I ever saw one although maybe not an intentional lie but certainly a flimsy truth that has been built on the strawless foundation of today's laughter and this afternoon's orgasms but I know better 'cause I have lived through the fiery wrecks of love gone bad and I've scoured the crash sites and I know that there are almost never any survivors

But even now while I am pushing her away in my mind our bodies move together like warm pacific tides and I fill her hips and fill her eyes and fill her moment with a joy that cannot be crucified by words or thought and I find myself wondering if it is really such a cold-blooded crime to try and stack love on good sex and eyes that give you hope in a hopeless world and my answer is that there are worse ways to coax love off the ground and even though I have personally picked through my share of relationship rubble looking for the black box that holds the pilot's miraculously calm voice saying Impossible To Maintain Altitude Please Assume The Crash Position her fingertips trace trembling circles around my nipples and I am almost ready to believe

And we hardly move hardly move at all 'cause we are both so very close and we want to make it last and preserve this precise instant when sex and sadness and melancholic lust sweeten the blood and the semen and the warm breath passed selflessly from each other's mouths 'cause this will be as close as we get to eden as close as we get to god and the sun before we begin our slow spiral descent oceanward dripping waxy feathers and we clutch at each other more tightly than ever before and for a brief moment we are victorious in stopping time stopping movement stopping the world from rolling forward stopping our ascent at its glorious apex but in the end we are just human and we are hungry and we are greedy and we cannot sustain god's greatness and so we move together once more once more into the breach and just before our shouted ecstasy will startle the world into lurching onward once again we understand understand without thinking that we have truly reached the Critical Moment when love is born to die

Save the Day

"Thank you, sir, you saved the day." The bag lady curled nicotine-stained fingers around the two quarters that were lastly mine and flashed a mouthful of street teeth, stubby and yellowed from eating soft, throwaway foods half-rotted behind grocery stores. No T-bones keeping her bicuspids sharp. She grinned up at me from the bus stop bench, blinking in the February sun like my old dog used to when I scratched his fattened belly. Made me feel almost like a big-timer at the track sliding neatly folded twenty-dollar bills into the breast pockets of grateful valets and bartenders and the old stable hands who talk to the horses like they're real friends and rub courage and speed back into their tired, trembling legs and shovel their steaming shit. Almost, but not quite.

I knew better. I had moved me a whole mountain range of horseshit down in Florida hooking up from small track to small track. Rubbed down a couple good horses along the way, but mostly stables full of bad ones. Weak ones. Thin racks of nervous muscle that twitched under the *buzz buzz buzz* of flies and crosshatched across the ass by the whip of the stick.

Every couple of months or so, one of them would break down in the middle of a race. You'd think you'd be able to hear a foreleg snap from a long way off, but the crack was always drowned out by the huzzahs of the sun-burned bettors and the thumping of hooves and crackling call of the loudspeaker reminding us — like we could ever forget — that Hot to Trot was out in front by a length, followed by the hard-charging trio of Finnigan's Fancy, Ride Sally Ride and Doppleganger's Double.

You never heard the leg snap, but the horse's scream was shrill, like steel train wheels braking hard.

And down they'd drop, like they'd been shot through the heart. The lucky jocks got tossed clear and escaped with maybe bruises, maybe a broken collarbone. Some got rolled on by their horse. I saw one poor jock, a Tijuana Mexican named Vasquez, break from the pack at the 3/4 pole. But his ride, a Kentucky chestnut called Baby Hughey, broke a leg coming out of the clubhouse turn where the leaky underground irrigation pipe soaks the track soft even in the middle of Sarasota's heat-baked August.

Vasquez was leaning hard, way out on the neck, pouring Spanish encouragement into Hughey's ear and pushing for the track record like he always liked to do. When the leg broke apart Vasquez fell under all that horse and got rolled bad. But the pack was coming hard, less than a length behind, and no one had time to steer clear. The Mexican got trampled by three other horses and pancaked by a fourth when it cartwheeled trying to jump over the wreck. Put Vasquez in a wheelchair so bad he couldn't even feed himself or change the bag they had draining his ass.

The track held a special night for Vasquez the following year and called it "Courage and Community" and looked to raise some money for him from the gate, but he never showed. Didn't blame him. It was a shithole. No place for a homecoming. Besides, after twenty years of whipping horses to victory, how happy can you pretend to be when they seat belt you into *that* life sentence?

And don't pay no mind to the old horsemen or ex-jocks on TV, horses aren't no friends, just horses, four-legged paychecks. Bad paychecks at that. Hardly enough to buy new shoes when the old ones split apart or food when the belly's hollowed out.

Yeah, in between jobs I scavenged the dumpsters, ate your castaway food. They say if you're gonna be a bum to do it somewhere warm so you don't wake up one morning with your nuts frozen to a grate. And that may be true, but the sun and heat can cook a man fast and sour food even faster. You gotta be quick on your toes down there 'cause you got your back up against a whole lot of down-and-out. Even the real crazy ones like Yellow John and Ricky Left Foot — poor bastards whose brains have been steamed soft from too much summer — even they know which restaurants offered the tastiest spoilage.

The first thing hunger devours is humanity. You'd turn the corner and trip over men rolling around in the dust, gouging eyes for yoghurt a week past its expiry date. Sometimes I'd keep living on not much more than black bananas and green bread and the hope of fatter times ahead. On good days, I'd strike it big on gag-sour chicken, burning away the hot rot on open fires down at the trainyards. A man can eat anything, all he needs is a little know-how and a great big hunger.

More often than not, The Life was all a man had. Even after his clean-shaven cousin tracked him down and cut him a fat check from a will drawn up back in Boise, Yellow John kept on bumming. "It's the only thing I do well," he said plain as spit, while we split a stash of half-gnawed rib bones behind a Hefty Heifer.

But that was then, a stretch of bad road that can happen to a person for no apparent reason other than bad luck or a coin toss that didn't go their way. The problem is, you never know how long that bad bit road will stretch or what the hell is waiting for you around the clubhouse turn. Look at Vasquez.

I heard how, after a whole series of painful surgeries, he learned to move well enough to blow out the pilot light of his mother's gas stove and twist the knob just enough to bring him some sort of lasting peace. Me? Sure, I had it tough for some years back then, but I've managed to keep my head above the sludge ever since. Found steady work and a handsome woman up north. She cooked us steak last night. T-bone.

I stood above that bag lady trying to guess how long she'd been out on the street. It's impossible to tell 'cause The Life will scuff you up real quick and paint you grey before you're ready.

I figured she was an old-timer. She smiled at the two bits I had flipped her way, but I recognized the terror stretched tight across her face. Terror, like I saw in Baby Hughey's eyes after he struggled upright on his three good legs, dangling the shredded fourth like a towel soaked in blood. Terror, like I saw when I grabbed the reins and held him steady as the track vet prepared the lethal injection. Terror, like I saw when the poison ran through his heart and dropped him where he shook. I never believed horses to be as smart as some people claim, but Baby Hughey knew something that day — knew he had run out of track.

I reached into my pocket and gave the sunburned old doll a twenty, unfolded. "Save the rest of the week too," I said and walked away, trying my best to ignore the sound of a train braking hard in the distance.

Salt

Having just finished shaving, Levi Walbourne looked out the window to check if the good weather had gained a foothold or not. For the past four days and nights an icy, black storm had assaulted the Newfoundland coast. Two storms in fact, one nipping maliciously at the ass of the other, swooping in from the Atlantic like Valkyries.

"Aw, Jesus H. Murphy." The woman heading up the walk meant trouble for sure. He could tell it by her determined stride and the set of her stubborn McCurty jaw. He heard firm resolve reverberate in the three sharp knocks that rattled his door. *Rap. Rap. Rap.*

Crossing the attic apartment, Levi wiped his hands with a towel and descended the cramped staircase leading to his place of business, Walbourne's Funeral Parlour. He flipped the towel over his shoulder and opened the door to be greeted by the stoic, wind-burned face of Adele McCurty.

"I'm here for the Old Man," she said. At 41, Adele was the eldest of the four McCurty girls and the one who most took after her grandfather, Titus. Standing 5' 10" she possessed the broad shoulders and thick wrists of a woman who had spent most of her life prying heavy gill nets and cod traps from the ocean. Back at the dock at the end of another day, Titus McCurty would light his pipe and grin with pride as he watched his granddaughter coil bulky rope or tinker with the cantankerous engine.

Levi shook his head. He spoke in the calm, low tones of a man who had been offering ineffective condolences to the bereaved for seventeen years. "I'm just going to get him ready now. You should come back when I'm done."

Adele loomed in the doorway, a full inch taller than Levi and just as wide through the chest. "If you don't mind, I'll fix him up myself," she said and stepped into threshold. He blocked her way with a hand against the sill. Her bosom pressed up against his forearm and Levi's angular face blushed red. "Actually, I do mind, Adele. This is my job. I'm sure you appreciate that."

She looked disdainfully at Levi's arm. "Maybe I'm not being clear enough here. I'm coming in and getting the Old Man ready. And I'll not be needing your blessing neither."

He had trouble holding her gaze. Ever since they were children sharing the desk by the stove at their tiny school-house Levi had been both repulsed and mesmerized by the strange masculine beauty of Adele's dark eyes.

They'd all walk home together, Adele and her sisters, and Levi and his two best friends, Ken Oake and Goward Welcome. Feeling full of himself one day, ten-year-old Goward tripped Adele's sister Connie, sending her sprawling into the wet grass.

Retribution was swift and sure. Levi didn't see the punch, but he'd never forgotten the image of Goward, his gang's Lancelot, arse in a mudhole, bawling into his palm as first, hot blood snaked between his fingers. Adele straddled the world above Goward saying nothing, just glaring down at him like winged vengeance.

Momentarily distracted by childhood recollections, Levi's gaze drifted to the stand of stunted black spruce that lined the road leading into town. Sensing an opening, Adele pushed through his arm like it was a turnstile, stopping to swipe away a glob of shaving cream from under his ear with her thumb.

Adele didn't ask where Titus' body was, she just marched straight to the back room. This was the only funeral home in Heart's Content, the only such establishment for 75 miles in either direction. There was none of the solemn formality found in a funeral home in St. John's or a big city on the mainland. During viewings people often went upstairs to use Levi's phone or change their babies' diapers on his kitchen table. On more than one hot summer day, he'd gone upstairs to find a couple of beers missing from his fridge. Levi sighed and followed Adele.

The day before, he had embalmed the cadaver on the stainless steel table in the corner, draining its blood and flushing its arteries, organs and thoracic cavity with preservatives and antiseptic agents. Now Titus lay on a padded table in the middle of the room illuminated by white fluorescent light.

Levi could never figure out why his father, Sam Walbourne, had invested in padded prep tables on which to shave and dress bodies — it wasn't as if comfort was much of an issue at this late hour of a person's day. Still, at that moment, with Adele looking down at the family's fallen patriarch, Levi was thankful for the comfort it might have afforded her. He was also glad that he had covered the body with a sheet. It was another habit he picked up from his father who believed that keeping corpses uncovered was disrespectful.

Levi hovered in the doorway a few feet behind Adele, his experience telling him not to interfere with these first intimate moments between the living and the dead. She stood at

Titus' side, affording Levi a good look at her profile. Her black hair was pulled back in a tight ponytail, just like she wore it almost every day of her life. High cheekbones ran brown and taut, intersected by a twenty-year-old jagged white scar where a careless knife had sliced her open when she was working as a dresser down at the fishing stage, knee-deep in dross, beheading cod and eviscerating them. Adele's full lips were pressed together as if she was trying to keep them from springing a leak and letting raw grief pour out into the open. Her black eyes were on Titus.

The summer before Levi had stared at his own father's body with those same eyes, knowing full well that death owned the day but still searching for the regular give-and-take of heart and lungs. Adele's brow knit tight as if she was trying to decipher the cryptic message that those with faith insist form the core of loss. She was looking for the sense of closure that Levi, one year into his own search, suspected never really comes.

An old, creased black purse, most probably not hers, swung from the crook of Adele's arm. Setting the bag down on the small ledge beside the prep table, she pulled out a black comb and a pair of scissors.

"Where do you keep your clean towels?" she asked over her shoulder. Levi pulled three towels out of a large cabinet and placed them on the table beside Titus. Adele gently lifted her grandfather's head, spread open a towel and laid him down upon the white.

Standing behind Titus, she slid the comb through his wiry hair. Her right hand combed and the left followed in its wake, ostensibly to flatten out stray grey strands, but caressing and anointing them at the same time. The comb hissed soft goodbyes as she pulled it toward her body. His few wild locks were properly subdued after just a few passes, but Adele kept grooming. After several minutes, she bent down over his flat, shiny hair and took a deep breath, just like she used to over the scraggly bouquets of dog violet, beach pea and devil's guts that she'd collect on their daily march to school. She looked up at Levi and smiled. "Salt."

Levi remembered leaning into his father's casket and being jarred by the sour tang of formaldehyde and germicidal soap. A lifetime of embalming had perfumed Sam's skin with such products, but they had always mingled with the fatherly scents of sweat and sandwiches and fertilizer from the garden. In death, those living smells had been obliterated. Levi decided to pass on shampooing Titus' hair.

The scissors clicked to life. It was obvious that Adele had cut a lot of hair, she moved like a barber, working the comb and scissors in perfect tandem. Grey cuttings peppered the towel. At 85, the old fisherman had little hair left, but Levi pictured him standing wide on the deck of *Safe Harbour II*, pipe in clenched teeth, with those long, unruly strands whipping in the wind like a skull and crossbones.

In a different time, in a different place, Titus McCurty could very well have been a buccaneer. He was a rogue — even by the fierce standards of seafarers — who was haunted by a restlessness that ebbed only when he was back on the roll of open water.

Titus was a legend. No one fished in deeper waters and no one stood their ground as long before turning shoreward to race ahead of howling, predatory storms. Some people, especially the more outspoken of the McCurty girls, called him reckless. Others believed he was a man of great courage. Still others considered him an arrogant tempter of fate. But none disputed his standing as the greatest sailor to ever captain a boat through that treacherous gauntlet of the North Atlantic.

But he also was the first man out on the water when boats broke apart on bloodthirsty nights and, no matter how big the seas, he was almost always the last man back home. On a dozen occasions he had charged headlong into squalls and plucked doomed sailors from the awful ocean. At least five babies in the area had been named Titus in honour of the man who had saved husbands, fathers and sons.

"If I nick him, will he bleed?" Adele stood over the stainless steel sink, deftly whipping up a lather in an old shaving mug. The brush's soft bristles were chewed short from years of puttying the crags of Titus' face.

Even after embalming there was always some residual blood left in a body, especially in the small capillaries near the surface. Levi nodded, "Yes, he'll bleed." She seemed relieved at the news. Her eyes softened as she smoothed the hot cream over Titus' face and neck with small, circular strokes, covering with white the thick red rut along his jawline where a German bullet grazed him in Beaumont-Hamel, France, in 1916.

Levi wondered if Titus had ever spoken to Adele about that horrific July 1st day when 800 stout-hearted sons of The Rock bravely went over the top straight into the chattering teeth of enemy fire. Within fifteen bloody minutes all but 68 were swallowed by the Somme, and even those who made it back alive and unwounded were never the same. Most lived out their lives wide-eyed and fearful, pissing their beds and crying for dead mothers during thunderstorms.

But Titus came back hard and angry, warring with the world like God Himself had promised tomorrow would never come. He squared off against everyone; shoremasters, crew members, fishery officials, even Johnny Micmac from the Conne River reservation down in Bay D'Espoir.

In winters he'd go near crazy waiting for the spring break-up to clear the harbour of ice. He'd load up a borrowed dogsled and disappear for weeks on end, locking himself away in a friend's shanty to poach at starving moose from the window. When a mainlander went missing from an ice-fishing camp back in '55 some whisperers told murderous tales of Titus and his black temper. People steered clear.

Levi walked over to the opposite side of the table. "Let me do his nails," he offered. Poised with a straight razor, Adele studied her grandfather's dirty, hard hands. They were the hands of a fisherman — stained with oil and cracked from exposure to wind, brine and sun. His nails were black and saw-toothed. Adele may have cut a lot of hair and shaved a lot of faces, but she hadn't given too many manicures. She nodded.

There were two flat pans just for this purpose. Levi filled both pans with hot water and solvent and lay Titus' hands in them. Half of his job was preparing a person for death by scrubbing away the traces of life.

Even through the blue film of soap, Levi could see Titus' wedding ring. Those hands had plunged a bayonet into the grey-clothed guts of a German boy, had fished through the fat times and the thin, had clung stubbornly to the wrecks of three boats, had hoisted newborn babies to the sun and shouldered old friends to their graves.

But through it all that gold band had stayed right there on his finger where, sixty-some-odd years ago, his bride Betty had slipped it on with a whispered vow of eternity.

Had the people of those parts been so metaphorically inclined they might have said that ring was the anchor that kept wild Titus McCurty from crashing on the rocks. That, and the girls.

Adele was the eldest of the four McCurty girls. Next came Molly and Constance — dubbed "the Irish Twins" by Titus because they were born just ten months apart — and, finally, baby Hope.

Of the sisters, only Adele had any recollection of their father, Simon. One of her most vivid memories of him was the day he let her turn the ignition on in one of the rusted clunkers he'd been eternally fixing up out back. Adele was almost six, and when the motor rumbled to life her father peeked out at her from around the hood with a smile that split open his boy's face. "Sonofabitch, Addy," he whooped, "you got the magic touch, girlie. We got ourselves a vehicle!" Jamming his face into the window, Simon greased his daughter's cheek with a kiss. Adele wrapped her arms around his neck, relishing one of those overwhelming waves of perfect love that stays with a person forever.

But less than two weeks later, Adele's dad drove off unannounced in the middle of the night, in that exact same junker — *their* junker. Big Bill O'Leary down at the ferry said that he last saw Simon heading east. Just another Newf following the Maritime trail of dreams down the Trans-Canada Highway to the big, landlocked cities far, far away from the sea. For her part, Adele was saddled with a child's guilt of having the magic touch that helped set those horrible wheels in motion.

Levi remembered the scandal. Adele was absent from school for weeks and all the adults were whispering sharply into each other's ears. As usual, he got his information from granny Carmichael, who loved nothing more than to sit in the chair by the window and tell the world what was happening in it. "That Simon never was no good," she croaked. "Not even a real man, just a boy who'd all haired up. Imagine, sneaking out like a snake and leaving behind a whole family." For weeks Levi would lie awake at night, praying to God that his father's car would still be there when he woke up.

And then there were the nights when he'd get torn from his sleep by nearby shotgun blasts. Titus would get drunk and stand on the bluff, cursing his own son's name and shooting holes in the ocean. Levi could never see him, but he could hear him screaming like a wild animal in a leg trap. "All his life, Titus has the devil tugging one arm and God t'other," granny Carmichael would say. "Mark my words, if the devil tugs hardest someone's gonna die before this muck settles." People started steering clear of Titus again.

But the devil must have given out first, because no one got killed. Three months to the day of his son's sudden departure, Titus rammed the trawler out into the surf, stabbing the ocean with his shame. He stayed out on the ocean for four days and three nights, radioing in once a day to say he was all right. A few boatloads of townspeople passed within 200 yards of Titus and reported back to the folks dockside how he was sitting on deck staring off into the Atlantic, engine cut. A ghost ship. "I ain't sure if he's eating, but he must be taking water," old Harry Neagle offered on the third day. "He had hisself a long leak offa the bow this morning."

Titus would never speak of the epiphanies he may have had out there in the deep water or what pacts were struck between fist-shaking man and his pantheon of flawed gods, but when he moored four days later Titus had changed. Calm and sober, he bent himself to the task of righting his son's wrong, taking in the four girls and their mother, Jen, and raising all five of them like they were his own daughters.

At Molly's sleeve-tugging request, Titus added a colourful corner of geraniums in the vegetable garden out back, kneeling in the dirt and yanking out weeds long after she had been distracted by a game of hide-and-seek. He couldn't read much, but he put the girls to bed every night with tales of his high sea adventures, embellishing them in some spots and, at Betty's insistence, censoring them in others.

Adele's favourite memories were of those summer mornings when the weather was friendly, and Titus would march down to the wharf with his crew of tiny pigtailed girls skipping behind him. He taught them how to tie bowline knots and prime the engine and how to chart a northeastern course using St. Anne's Church on Fogo Island as their reference point. By the time Baby Hope was six, all four girls could mend coarse nets and guide a trawler to the Grand Banks' fishing grounds where the big schools ran thick.

For their part, the girls took great pleasure in making their grandfather laugh and clap, staging puppet shows in the wheelhouse. Pricky, woollen socks were magically transformed into knights and kelp-haired princesses who seemed forever in flight from huge, scaly dragons — dragons that looked suspiciously like big, fat cod heads stuck on the end of a gaffing iron. A natural mimic, Adele would make Titus howl with her impersonations of Joe Bantry, slicking her hair down in a shameless comb-over and rising up on her toes as she plucked the underwear out from her arse.

But as they grew older, the girls found other, more traditional interests. All, except Adele. She abandoned high school and, ignoring her mother's strenuous objections, begged her way aboard the trawler to work full-time beside her grandfather. While her sisters were getting married and raising boisterous young families, Adele fell in love with the wordless mysteries of the ocean.

She went out with Ken Oake for some eight months after he had come back from teacher's college. Often the gang of them would go out, Levi and Sheila, Goward and Helen, and Ken and Adele. They were all in their early twenties at the time and their nights were full of beer and belly laughs. But even though she was happy and sociable, Adele always seemed happiest to watch from the corners. Sometimes she'd catch Levi looking at her and she'd smile and hold his eyes until he looked away.

"She's a fucking mystery wrapped in an enigma, all right," Ken muttered to Levi, as he was packing to go teach in a military college in Kingston. Earlier that day, Ken had asked Adele to go with him; he'd be making enough money to support them both until she found a job. "She didn't even say a word. Just kissed me on my forehead and left. On my fucking forehead!" He laughed bitterly and shook his head. "And then I watched her out the window and, you know what? She walked straight down to the water and took the boat out. Perfect Adele."

Levi put his hand on his friend's shoulder. Ken was hurt and confused, unable to rely on logic to solve Adele. He loved Ken and wanted him to be happy, but try as he might, Levi just couldn't picture Adele working behind a counter in Kingston. She belonged on the water. Perfect Adele.

The razor dragged deliberately along Titus' jaw. So slow that Levi could hear the crackling of individual hairs as they were sheared away. Adele used upward strokes, making sure her grandfather's last shave would be his closest. It was a face she knew well, skillfully navigating the moles that lurked shoal-like beneath the creamy, white froth. When she got to his jowls she paused. "The Old Man would puff his cheek for me," she said without looking up. No breath left in him now.

Adele drew the sinewy skin on his neck taut by pulling back on his chin. That her hands were elegant and graceful surprised Levi who had assumed they'd be as knotty and muscular as the bloodless pair he now worked on. He trimmed black, crescent moons from Titus' yellow fingernails all the while admiring Adele from out of the corner of his eye.

They worked in silence. The more he watched Adele the more he was struck by the divine simplicity in the way she touched Titus. Levi knew that aside from Betty, none of their family ever much attended church. Adele least of all. However, it was clear that she was administering her own last rites, cleansing the mortal body in preparation for its last moments on sunlit earth. A granddaughter's final benediction of the man who had raised her. A sailor's last blessing for the Old Man.

Levi loved that term, Old Man, as it is used by sailors. It's the title that mariners have bestowed upon their captains for centuries. Simple and honest, it is both a term of endearment and a sign of respect for the wisdom and courage a man must possess to grow old on an ocean that so readily feeds on young men.

When she finished shaving, Adele washed Titus' face with the clean towel. Gazing upon her handiwork, she noticed something, picked up the scissors again and delicately trimmed the coarse black hairs that sprouted from his nose and ears. She looked at his hands, cleaned, dried and lying by his side, and nodded her approval. Bending over, she whispered love and farewells into Titus' ear and pressed her lips down upon on his bony forehead. Her hand lay on his chest where his strong heart once raced with the waves. Reaching behind her, she unclasped a small pendant and secured it around his neck.

In his line of work, Levi had seen his fair share of religious icons but for some reason it surprised him that Adele, so wild and independent, would own such a necklace. He tried to squint away his myopia and identify the saint embossed on the medallion. Fishermen have a handful of patron saints looking out for them from above and Levi was sure it was one of the more popular ones: Andrew or Peter. Maybe even Nicholas or Zenos.

Adele saw him straining to see and rolled her eyes with a small exasperated smile that she had kept since childhood. "Magnus, Levi. It's Magnus." Magnus, yes, of course. The fearsome Viking chief and pirate who gave up his heathen ways to convert to Christianity. He couldn't help but grin.

Both the medallion and the wedding band refracted the sterile white light into lively glints of gold. Levi realized Titus wasn't like most of the dead he had prepared before. His father, as good a funeral man as there was on the coast, had quietly lamented how the deceased never look quite right, not like they did when they were alive.

There were any manner of things that could go wrong; flushing the body too quickly during embalming could cause the face to puff and swell; an incorrect set of the mouth could add an uncharacteristic scowl; and too much makeup would give the cheeks the appearance of polished apples. But even beyond these technical pitfalls, death wrenched something away on last breath. Something invisible but of great physical substance.

Despite his father's great talent and innate respect for the dead, they always came out looking no better than skillful reproductions of the original model. One night, just a few weeks before his own sudden death, Sam confided in his son that he dreaded nothing more than a family's first viewing of a loved one. "I see it in their faces, especially the children. Disappointment like we've stolen away their father or mother. You know, there was a time when families buried their own dead." He leaned his head back and sighed. "Maybe they were right not to trust outsiders with so intimate a task."

Yes, maybe they were right. Lying there, just two days away from internment, Titus looked like Titus — haughty and defiant even after being swallowed up by the one storm no sailor can outrun. Somehow Adele's familiar hands had infused his flat, breathless corpse with fullness. She knew her grandfather better than anyone. Betty may have been married to him for all those years, but they were landlocked moments and tethered passions. Adele was by his side on the water, when he was free to rage and whoop and challenge the forces that towered over the world. Under his granddaughter's touch Titus looked restless again, an uncooperative corpse straining at its own finite bonds. A Viking chief on the funeral pyre.

Her task completed, Adele hung like a ghost beneath the harsh light. Her strong body suddenly looked as though it could crumble into dust, as if she had transferred all her vitality back to its source in Titus. It reminded Levi that the other half of his job was attending to the living. "Do you want to sit, Adele? Can I get you some water?" He put his hand on her shoulder and pointed to the couch in the hallway outside.

She shook her head. "No, thank you. I gotta be off and get myself ready for the guests."

"You look exhausted."

"I guess I am," she said looking down, ashamed of her weakness. Titus. "Didn't feel it until now. I couldn't sleep much last night for all the crying in the house. And even when it quieted down I couldn't sleep again. I couldn't cry neither. Too jumpy, you know?" She paused and smoothed the sides of her black dress with her hands. Adele was never easy with her words.

"In the middle of the night I got out of bed and was gonna get out on the water, but when I passed his room I crawled into his empty bed instead. I sunk right in the sag in the middle and it made me think about him in that box all squeezed in underground forever. Made me scared." She reached out and ran trembling fingertips across Titus's eyelids. Levi fought the urge to interject some impotent expression of support and sympathy. "Let the living have their say," his father had advised.

"Then I remembered something the Old Man told me a long time back. I was just a girl and we were coming back in, just off Random Island. It was right after Whitey got drowned, remember?"

Yes, he remembered all too well. Vaino "Whitey" Kärkkäinen was an albino who had moved to Heart's Content from some big city in Finland, maybe Helsinki. Those same whisperers had him running from something, sometimes from the law, sometimes a broken heart.

Whitey was a giant man — "wide as the devil's boots," Dorman Hawk would crow — with a giant laugh. He was often spotted walking and arguing with Titus, all four girls perched across his shoulders like chirpy sparrows on a line.

Whitey caught a freak storm down near Burnt Islands. Titus helped fish the corpses of the seven crew out of the frigid water but couldn't find his friend. He stayed out on the water all night until the wet and cold had chewed right through him and saddled him with a pneumonia that scarred his lungs forever. Three weeks later, Whitey's huge pink body washed up down near Mystic in Connecticut, having rode the Labrador Current thousands of miles down the East Coast.

"I was young and I didn't know anything about that stuff. Death, you know? I asked him how come they found all the others right away but not Whitey. And he told me about how the ocean'll grab some people, the good ones, and keep them for a spell — but once it takes what it needs, it gives them right back.

"Said it was the same with the earth. Said when you bury a person they get swallowed to where it's all fire and lava. Said the earth needs us like fuel." Adele's voice trembled and she was leaning on Titus for support. Her eyes never left her grandfather.

"And then, when the earth is full, full of life, it bubbles and bubbles and a volcano blows off somewhere, you know? And it shoots all that dirt and fire and life into the sky. Said that it gets all scattered by the wind and settles around the world — sometimes as far off as Japan and Fiji. But sometimes right here at home."

Levi thought of Titus railing away in the belly of some far-off geyser or volcano, demanding his release. "Oh he'd get spit out soon enough," he thought to himself with a smile. Adele looked up at Levi. She was crying but her eyes were brave again. "And thinking about what he said made me feel good. Thinking about him and me and the girls on the boat making puppet plays. I could smell the Old Man on the pillows, Levi, and it made my body feel right in that sag."

Levi reached over and cupped her elbow. This time she looked at his hand and smiled. Then she took him in her arms and hugged him hard. He had held many trembling mourners before, offering them his unspoken support and propping them up until they found their legs again. But Adele felt strong — open wide to her grief but unbowed by it. Defiant again.

"Thank you, Levi," she whispered, pressing the side of her face against his. He kissed her cheek tenderly. Her hot tears burned his lips and seeped into his mouth, filling it with a taste he would forever equate with love. Salt.

Bread Crumbs
and Band Saws

My old man has always been a firm believer that kids should start working fairly early in life. Nothing crazy — no carpet weaving or cabin boy crap — just menial summer jobs that paid minimum wage. He thought that it would teach us about the value of money and all that sort of stuff that adults just can't wait for kids to learn.

When I was fourteen, I killed the summer working in the warehouse owned by one of his drinking pals. It was pretty slack, just filling out orders, boxing them up and completing the invoices. Aside from having to punch in at 7 a.m., I thought it was a pretty neat gig. The guys I worked with were all older, but they treated me like an adult — except for the time they mummified me with a tape gun, boxed me and left me in the accountant's office for him to discover later that morning.

In some ways dad was right, the job gave me my first taste of financial freedom. I was the first one of my gang who had a ready supply of cash and this dovetailed seamlessly with our collective discovery of beer as a recreational activity. Plus, it was an athletic supply warehouse so I was always able to steal some top-flight shorts and track suits.

But my work life, especially the manual labour side of things, went steadily downhill soon after that. A few years after the warehouse job, I found myself toiling in a machine shop in an industrial section of Montreal.

I busted my hump there for three straight summers, sweating until the oil trickled down my ass crack and learning everything a boy could learn about the mundane world of pipe fittings. It was a filthy job. At the end of each shift my earplugs were slick with black waxy film and my hands looked like they belonged on a Welsh miner. Blowing my nose just yanked up more dark gunk from some once-pink corner of my soul. My old man believed these kinds of jobs were character building. I don't know if my character got any stronger but, for the first time in my life, I couldn't wait for school to start in the fall.

For most of my sentence in the machine shop I was plopped in front of a big hydraulic press, squeezing pipe into elbow joints. It was hot, greasy and loud like an airport runway. A few years after I had moved on to another shit job my younger brother inherited my press and promptly squeezed a finger clear off. It was also mildly dangerous.

When guys went on vacation in the summer, I usually was the one who replaced them. Sometimes, like when Charley in the stockroom was gone, it was a sweet and easy respite from shop floor purgatory. He had a little office that boxed out the white noise, complete with chairs with padded armrests and a stash of skin mags in the bottom drawer. He also kept a small bottle of rye down there, but I noticed the level hardly went down from one year to the next. Later in life I would learn that sometimes just knowing it's there is comfort enough.

In general, however, replacement work was always bad. Without a doubt, the worst was when Lucky the Polack went fishing with his beloved son near North Bay for three weeks and I had to take over on his goddamned band saw.

Take my word for it, there is nothing more terrifying than feeding sheet metal through an old, pre-safety standards industrial band saw. The blade is just a 20-foot loop of shark teeth gnawing the air at 100 miles an hour. There is a hospital smack dab in the centre of this little corridor of industry that is full of screaming machinists clutching at stumps of fingers, hands and arms. Most have been mauled by band saws exactly like Lucky's.

The problem with the old band saws is this: when it comes down to the precision cuts you've got to use your hands to guide whatever it is you're cutting. The stick or featherboard that you use to push for the rough cuts just doesn't give you the right kind of play or accuracy.

And, Christ, it always seemed like Lucky saved all the precision cuts for me. He'd be there, two weeks before he was leaving, smiling and waving to me from across the shop while he cut up the big chunks of bulk steel. But the pile of pipe fittings that needed to be shaved down just right never got any smaller. Lucky wasn't lucky, just smart. Losing your casting thumb is the quickest way to spoil a fishing trip.

Of course, by that stage of his life Lucky was running low on body parts. Over the years, he had lopped off the pinkie of his right hand, and the first two fingers of his left hand were chewed right down to the second joint. His standard joke was to stick the remaining nub of his index finger in his ear or nose and wince like he had jabbed a whole digit straight into his brain. Nobody on the floor laughed anymore except Lucky. He'd slap his ass and do some crazy Polish jig with his bandy little legs.

The days leading up to Lucky's departure filled me with dread. All I could think about was me hunched over his fucking saw, eyes and fingers and all kinds of soft, fat veins just inches from the blade. Just slicing off a centimetre of pipe and praying that nothing slipped, praying that I'd punch out with all my parts. The only thing that buoyed my spirits was daydreaming about Lucky buzzing off another knuckle. I could almost hear him howling Polish curses and spraying blood like some Monty Python sketch.

None of the regular guys much liked Lucky. They grumbled that he was moody and if the mood was a pissy one he was hell to work with. If he was feeling mean and you asked him to rush a batch of pipe because the boss was leaning on you, he'd jut out his chin with a sneer and insist that your order had to take its place in line like all the others. A lot of the old-timers liked playing lord of their concrete patch of floor, but Lucky strutted around like Henry VIII himself.

And everyone would always blame Lucky if any tools or material went missing. A moon-faced pack rat, he was always rooting through the scrap pile for bent pieces of sheet metal and the like that he could use at home. Jesse the Floor Boss, the only man who had been to Lucky's home, said it was a patchwork quilt of rough-cut steel and wood from broken pallets. A banged-up gingerbread house of bent tin and splintered wood. It was as if he was exacting revenge on all the shops that had stolen most of his parts.

Lucky was good enough to us summer guys, though. Sometimes a little too nice. He was always goosing your ass when you were bent over picking up a heavy cast iron die, or *tap tap tapping* your nuts with the back of his gloved hand when you were wiping sweat from your eyes. The French boys all claimed he was queer, but I never believed that shit. After all, his wife would pick him up every payday so they could do the groceries.

Of course, even she didn't seem to be very fond of Lucky. Every time she drove up to the shop she'd just stand by the open loading dock door with her hands on her hips looking mightily put out. She'd never come all the way in, like she was scared she'd oil up her ruby slippers. She was younger than him, but she was hard around her lips and eyes, kinda like what happened to Nadia Comaneci when she got tainted with age. And she had that bad Eastern European fashion sense — too much makeup and lots of tight, rhinestoned clothes that only accentuated her growing little gut.

I never saw Lucky in anything other than his green work clothes and the old bandana he knotted around his bald head, but she was always wrapped up in something new and spangled. He liked to crow about how passionate she was, but my later experience with women like her taught me that they never give anything up for free.

As soon as Lucky caught a glimpse of his wife scowling in the doorway, he'd yoo-hoo with a wave, beetle over to the locker room and wash up in two minutes flat.

Most of the time she'd start giving him shit the second he got to within ten feet. I couldn't hear what she was saying over the blast of the machines, but it was plain for all to see that she relished bitching him out in public.

Often Lucky's son slouched in the back of the car, brooding as usual for having to waste his precious time helping his dad lug the groceries. Lucky was always yammering on about the boy-wonder, about how he was going to be a heart doctor one day and what a good, attentive son he was. I later found out that the punk decided to skip the fishing trip at the last minute just to see some concert with his friends. Lucky ended up going alone.

The week before Lucky packed his rod and reel I was anchored beside him, watching him put the saw through its paces. He briefed me on everything; how to feed sheet metal into the saw so it wouldn't twist; how to keep the small lubrication nozzle from clogging with tiny metal burrs; and how to tighten the saw just right depending on what material you were cutting. "Blade tension very important," he'd say in his Pidgin English. "Too loose makes crooked cut, too tight makes broken blade." I listened like an intern in the operating room, fully aware that the life I could be saving would be my own.

Believe me, nothing'll make you shit your pants with more conviction than a snapped blade. See, all man-made things have their imperfections. Every chain, every car, every loving relationship has a built-in weakness just waiting to blow. These blades have maybe 1,000 teeth on them, maybe 5,000, and, through use, they wear down and snap off. One or two here or there doesn't make a difference, but sometimes it starts a whole chain reaction and dozens of them start flying at you — diamond-tipped shrapnel whizzing through the air looking for a nice flesh landing pad. If too many teeth get sheared off, the blade weakens and, if you don't shut her down straight away, the whole loop snaps soon after.

It only lasts a second — a busted blade will do one revolution before clattering to the ground — but it is the most frightening second on earth. I'd rather butt out a cigarette on a pit bull's balls than wrangle with an out-of-control saw. It's scary enough when the damn thing is running smoothly in its track, but try to imagine what kind of malicious motherfucker it is when it breaks free. Nothing more than a steel bullwhip looking for blood. Lucky has a thick, knotted scar slashing across his back and neck courtesy of a broken blade. Carved clean through his muscles and tendons in his right shoulder. Almost lost the whole damn arm right there on the shop floor.

One day, a bunch of the boys went to a nearby strip joint for the free lunch buffet, or "muff-et," as they called it. I got left behind because I was underage and François the Welder was scared we'd all get busted or something. The boys would whisper how François had spent sixteen months in prison for putting the beats on a teacher back when he was a teenager. They said he had a smart mouth and a bullhead, and the combo made for lots of wrangles with the guards. He still walks with a limp from one of the times they really busted him up. I guess he had reason to be wary of the boys in blue.

Lucky was pretty Old World, meaning he didn't believe in watching women dance naked. The closest he came to porn was an antique centrefold hanging in his locker. It was real vintage stuff, some fleshy blonde with a beehive hairdo sporting an old-style bikini bottom and sticking her fat white tits at the camera.

As it was, it was just me and Lucky in the lunchroom. I had finished my ham sandwich and was leaning against the wall on the back two legs of my chair. I was daydreaming about winning an Olympic medal in something. Anything. Lucky was carving the peel off a sour-looking apple with the knife that he kept in his pocket.

Christ, he looked like every puffy-chested Polish dock worker you've ever seen standing in the background behind Lech Walesa. He was medium-sized, but thick and powerful across the shoulders and through the wrists and what was left of his hands. Even though he was putting on weight, he still had knobby cheekbones butting out from his round face. His most prized possession was his gold tooth. "In Poland now, they kill me for my mouth," he'd grin. "Bandits everywhere."

He started talking about his father, Jozef, told me that he never really knew him because he was killed at the beginning of World War II. "I was just baby boy, but I have his uniform and sword in here," he said, pointing to his head.

Lucky's dad was in something called the Pomorske Cavalry Brigade. Jozef and over 300 fellow cavalrymen were killed in a single battle in 1939 while trying to defend the Pomeranian Corridor against the onrushing Nazis. Hitler was in a dead sprint to capture Warsaw before the rest of the world finally woke up and caught a whiff of the totalitarian coffee.

This was early in the war and little was known about the Nazis' power and their advanced weaponry. Riding their snorting Arabians over the crest of a hill, Jozef and the others must have felt their hearts screech to a stop when they saw column after armoured column of German Panzer tanks rolling toward them across the fields in their inexorable march to the capital.

But, scared or not, those Polish sonofabitches didn't flinch, not for a second. Duty was duty and theirs was to protect the homeland. Undaunted, the officers drew their curved sabres and gave the order to charge.

And charge they did. Down from the hill galloped the doomed brigade, closer and closer, until the pounding of the hooves was swallowed by the mechanical thunder of tanks that churned their farms into dust. They leaned into their ride, shouting "Freedom!" against the crisp September wind and thrusting their swords toward the cogged heart of each Panzer.

But they never made it to within a football field of a single enemy soldier. The tanks and mounted guns blew horse and brave man into bloody, pulpy bits, blew them into death, exploded them into legend. "The Nazis never stop," said a grim-faced Lucky. "Drive over everything, crush everything alive and dead."

I had heard of the Polish cavalry's heroic charge from my brother the war nut, but he said that it was more myth than fact. Lucky took out a photo from his wallet, a small brown photo of a man in a dark wool uniform sitting proudly on a muscular black horse. He has one hand on the handle of his sabre and the other on the reigns. Jozef had haughty eyes that probably *could* stare into the muzzle of a Panzer and still spur his horse onward.

Just then, the door to the lunchroom burst open and the boys jumbled in, laughing and backslapping and waxing blue-collar poetic about the heart-shaped ass on a peeler named Tiffany. Lucky pushed himself up from the table with weary arms. I followed him to the floor and watched him shuffle over to the saw. He was getting old and his body was starting to break apart, starting to chip away, fingertip by fingertip.

Maybe his father was the lucky one, blown right out of here in one mighty cataclysmic moment and ground back into his native soil under relentless Nazi treads. Lucky was a million miles from home, and he had left nothing behind but a pitiful trail of lopped-off body parts — bloody bread crumbs in the grimmest of all fairy tales — to trace his insignificant machine-shop history. Parts that have been swept up with the dust and metal bits at the end of each shift and thrown in the big green dumpsters out back.

Jozef was a hero, a folk song, a legend that got bigger with each telling. Lucky, on the other hand, was getting smaller with each punch of the clock. He was fighting a much different war, a war of protracted attrition. What the band saw didn't take outright, his wife and son would wear away, trading feigned affection for alligator handbags and fat anatomy textbooks.

The shop floor was dead quiet as the other men got into place and screwed their earplugs back into their heads. A cool breeze blew through the open loading dock door and rolled across the floor. It was peaceful like it is in movies before armies collide. The guys stood motionless in front of their machines, clinging to the last silent moments before they were obliterated again by heat and white noise. The old band saw screamed to life a full minute before the whistle sounded to mark the end of lunch and everyone's head turned. Brandishing nothing but a thin length of steel in front of himself, Lucky walked straight toward those horrible spinning teeth.

Making It

Trixie had a beauty mark under the outside corner of her left eye that looked like one of those painted-on mime's tears. Marcel Marceau. No matter how happy she was — and she's one of the most effervescent people I have ever met — that tiny tear, suspended perfectly and forever, always made her look like she was crying. Hell, even when Trixie was hollering an endless string of orgasms into the lucky night, that small tear tinged it all with a sweet melancholy that I revered.

See, my father was a dreamer who always hung his brass rings way too high. He was cursed with big vision and short, alligator-arm reach. He'd sit on the porch on the sunniest days listening to Billie Holiday, searching the obits for names of friends, and kicking around titles for his Great Canadian Novel. Titles for three-paragraph books that were never finished.

My ma's childhood dream of having a big boisterous family died with the arrival of her first child. That ghastly day she gave birth to a premature runt with a hole in his heart along with almost half her blood. The doctors sewed me up and tied her shut, and although she has never spoken a single word of it to me, every time she hugs me I feel her thin arms course with love and grief, regret and forgiveness. Feel her squeeze it right into me. With a melancholic bloodline like that it was inevitable that I fell in love with Trixie and her exquisitely doleful tear.

Trixie was born way up in the Gaspé, in some tiny little four-house outpost. Not even a dot on the map, and a long way from my cosmopolitan smugness. When we first met I was flitting around on gossamer wings, tweaking my thesis and oozing one part intellect and three parts bullshit. I thought I was such a brilliant man, so well read and well travelled. A big city big shot who looked at her as a loveable hillbilly. A reclamation project. My own Eliza Doolittle.

But now I realize that she was so much more than me, that every important lesson I learned as an adult didn't come from books; they came from her. Until we met, I was just words, but Trixie was action and sweet adventure. While I sat and ruminated on the theories of living, she was out there doing it big, doing it hard, just kissing and dancing and drinking with friends, lovers and fortunate strangers.

Watching her work a room became one of my greatest joys. She'd bust through the door like an ass-wiggling fireball and light the place up. A Roman candle on legs. People sought her out like cripples on a faith healer. They just wanted to be next to her and bask a little, kiss the hem of her dress. And there was no greater feeling than making her happy. Great big belly laughs rolling through the crowd like a warm breeze laden with pollen and seeds and all that life-giving stuff that feeds us all — even us unfortunates locked away in our sealed emotional vaults.

Christ, which one of heaven's blacksmiths forged that marvellous laugh? Red-hot and happy, it glowed on the anvil as Divine muscles shaped it with ringing swings of the hammer. *Ding ding ding.* Church bells calling true believers to Mass. The first time I heard Trixie laugh I thought back to my summers as a kid on Lake Memphremagog when we stayed at Irish Tom's cottage. At night the waves rocked the small sailboat moored on the dock and made the halyards slap against the metal mast — *ding ding ding* — lulling me to deep, trusting sleep.

Trixie and I did a lot of celebrating in the nine years we lived together. She was a boisterous hunk of life whose body was ferociously made. Hips that rolled like big Pacific waves and jutting breasts that she'd push up against me when we fought. We'd snarl and spit at each other like badgers and then fuck our way back into love and gracefulness.

That woman almost made me lose two jobs just by hypnotizing me in bed. Couldn't bring myself to wriggle free from the cling of her legs and arms and siren song. Sweet shit, one taste of her wine-dipped lips and even the most dedicated postman would miss his appointed rounds. She had an open-mouthed smile that would swallow all my sadness, all my melancholy, and fend off the teeth-gnashing nastiness that crouched in wait for me just outside our thin door. Just the sound of her whispered voice on the other end of the phone would wrangle a shaft of life from even my darkest mood.

I needed a pedestal on which to balance her miraculous form, but I couldn't bear the thought of exposing her to the elements and jealous eyes and Shakespeare's slings and arrows. Instead, I shielded her behind my rhino-skinned self and deflected whatever poison-tipped darts came hissing at her propelled by malice or just dumb chance. She didn't really need my protection, but it made me feel safer to cloak her in my contempt for the outside world.

One day, we were walking down Sherbrooke Street smiling at kids and scratching the bellies of mongrel dogs. I was striding like the big winners do down at the track, waving to bus drivers and magnanimously flipping my spare change to the bums. We were halfway across a street when a car veered around the corner and almost clipped Trixie. I was filled with a rage that I'd never felt before. I howled and gave chase to the bastard vehicle. I hurled our bum money at it, pinging and zinging it off the back window, trunk, and bumper.

The car screeched to a stop and an irate face frowned from the side mirror. A young man, thick of neck and furrowed of brow, unclipped his seat belt. He was twice my size and he looked like a real meat-eater. But before he could open his door, I shattered that mirror with one clumsy boot from my clumsy boot. I pounded the hood with my fists. I slobbered on the windshield. I foamed at the mouth. I spoke in tongues. I grabbed the broken side mirror and hammered craters in the door. My eyes bulged. My teeth gnashed. A tiny rivulet of blood drip drip dripped from my nose. Then I grabbed the door handle.

He slammed the lock down. Young bull-necked men fear no man — except the truly insane. Can't hit the madman, everyone knows it'll bring bad luck. He stomped on the gas and careened down the street, almost tearing off my left hand at the root.

Sweet Christ, I never felt so good. Who would have thought that senseless violence could zap you full of life like that? It sure beat the shit out of any adrenaline rush I'd ever gotten on the badminton court or parsing sentences. I hopped up and down and shook my throbbing fist at the prick. Rage exploded in my eyes like Chinese fireworks and I was hepped up for more. But when I saw Trixie leaning on a mailbox and dangling that crooked smile of hers at me, my anger welled up inside the ball of blood hanging off my nose and toppled harmlessly to the ground.

I whooped and jumped to click my heels in victory and crashed to the ground with a fat-assed splat. Giggling, Trixie rushed to help me up off the asphalt just as a man in a van started leaning on his horn. I brandished my trusty mirror with menace and flashed my canines at the Van Man. Having had her fill of my puffy-chested posturing, she yanked me to the curb by my ear. "That's enough windmills for today," she laughed, dabbing my nose with the cuff of her old sweatshirt.

"Anything you say, Sweet Sancho," I smiled, wrapping my arms around her and giving that perfect left ass cheek a comforting squeeze. She buried her face in my chest, pressing the side of her face against the scar that marked my faulty heart. But on that day my heart beat big and it poured grateful love into her ear, thanking her for making me feel strong and whole. Grateful, for the first time, for being born.

One of the bums on a bench gave me a thumbs-up and a gappy jack-o'-lantern grin, like I was one of his sunburned gang who had made it. Returning the thumbs-up with a grin, I felt like I finally had.

Dark Girl

It's Sunday afternoon and I'm perched on a rock on a riverbank outside of Quebec City. In the water, a few feet in front of me, stands the most beautiful woman I know, though I really don't know her very well.

She is wearing nothing but a sports bra and a pair of black shorts hiked up past the hard swoop of her ass cheek. She is just standing there, hands on her hips, water lapping at her curves, trying to soak away the stiffness in her legs. Saturday is rugby day. Sunday is the day she asks the river to whisk away the pain. Me? I just gobble aspirin and beer.

The day before, we had agreed to meet and take a stroll by the city's Old Port. We ate ice cream on a pier and tossed the bottom nub of our cones into the water for the fat, squawking seagulls. The sun was unseasonably hot and we were sweating. Still licking the drippy vanilla ice cream off of her wrist, she suggested we drive to the river, to a place she claimed almost nobody knew about. The thought of a swim was appealing, even though it was mid-May and she had cautioned that the water would be cold.

Christ, is it cold. Too cold for me to venture out even a few feet. I dip my foot in and yank it back with a yelp. Instead, I settle down on a cool ledge of stone and tuck my knees up under my chin. I press the towels against my chest, letting my heart beat into the soft cotton. She wades out, fearlessly ignoring the cold's bite simply because she had told me that she was going in.

Further down river the terrain is more level and there are sandy shoals where people like to gather to sunbathe and gossip and drink the beer that they keep submerged under water. Where she has led me, however, the banks are very steep, making it difficult to get to. We are alone, me and the most beautiful woman I know.

If you saw her, you would bet all your father's money she's an Indian. She has long black hair pulled back in a shiny ponytail and nut-brown skin even in the midst of sunless February. She has the high, sharp cheekbones and proud eyes that you only find on Walt Disney Indians, when Uncle Walt is being kind with his racial stereotyping.

But she's not Indian at all. Her mother is French Canadian and her father is from France. He's Basque, which makes sense, because the only other Basque I know is dark and foreboding too.

The first time I saw this girl, she was coming off the rugby field after a loss. She stomped right past me, furious at herself for only scoring twice. Her black eyes flashed like an eagle's or those of Rocket Richard when he swooped in on a breakaway. It made me think of a storm I once saw whipping across Lake Memphremagog straight toward my family's cottage. It was a stunning sight; a huge black spider crawling across the water on lightning-bolt legs. But I was a boy and it frightened me. I hid in my mother's arms.

This woman's body is sleek and lithe. The perfect muscles in her arms and shoulders ball up and release when she rappels down the riverbank on creepers and roots exposed by erosion. I can't help but wonder what it would be like to feel her body press against mine, to give myself up to the storm instead of running from it.

I help coach a women's rugby team in Montreal and most of the players live there year-round. The squad is a weird and wonderful mix of people; Anglos and Francophones, women from B.C. and Manitoba, France and New Zealand and a pair from the States. Aside from rugby, their only common trait is that, for whatever reason, they have all ended up in Montreal. All, except her. She lives near Quebec City, and, typical of her stubborn resolve, she refuses to move in with a teammate for the summer rugby season. Instead, she commutes the 200 miles twice a week in her rusty old Chevette, once for Thursday practice and once again for Saturday's game.

She doesn't trust Montreal, doesn't trust its size and pace. The absence of forests and lakes make her feel uneasy. She needs horizons, nature's irregular curves. She's better off here in her secret place, safe in the elbow of this river. I can see that by the way her body mimics the current's give-and-take, swaying slightly, a tree in the wind. I hear my grandfather's voice counselling me that staking a sapling to make it grow straight will, in the end, just weaken it.

Many of the French girls on the team are good friends of hers from back in the days when they all played on the same team up here. But most of them turned their strong backs on rural Quebec to chase careers and excitement in cosmopolitan Montreal.

When she isn't around they talk about her and her rough ways with a grin and a shake of the head. Watching her spoon handfuls of cold water over her smooth brown shoulders I am reminded of the gold dredged up in old miners' pans and I finally realize what her friends mean when they say she is *"un peu sauvage,"* slightly savage. It isn't an insult at all; they just know what I have only now come to understand — that she will be forever unpolished, a raw gemstone given up by the loving earth.

Later, when she has waded back to shore and sat down beside me, we talk a bit. But never so much as to disturb the river's tranquillity. Our words come out in small whispered clutches, not any louder or more obtrusive than the small black-winged grackle gliding from bank to bank in search of shadflies to feast upon.

She tells me how once she was sitting on a bus when she realized that a small girl clutching a Pocahontas lunchbox was staring up at her, mouth agape. The girl looked at the box and then at this beautiful woman in amazement. When the child and her mother got up to leave, she touched the girl's shoulder and said with a wink, "I'm Pocahontas, who are you?"

"Giselle," the girl whispered, eyes wide like bronze medals.

"Have a nice day, Giselle," she said, smiling as the awe-struck child was led out of the bus swinging her lunchbox.

But on this day Pocahontas has legs that are bruised and battered. She is not the biggest woman going, not by a long shot, but she plays rugby with pure ferocity, like she's going into war. Like she's going into love. And the other women on the team follow on her winged heels, screaming into battle, inspired by her courage and unflinching commitment. Amazons, all, for a day.

I ask about a scar slashing across her knee and she tells me how she split her kneecap in half while skiing when she was thirteen. "Does it bother you when you play?" I ask. She smiles very softly, happy, I can tell, for my concern. "No, the doctors did a good job." She guides my fingertips over the scar, white as my Irish skin. "See? Just a small bump." Her hands are cold from the water's chill and I realize that this is the first time I've touched her.

We talk about jobs. In my tortured French I list my string of minimum wage dead-enders that finally led to my getting shunted behind a computer. Warehouses, moving companies, bottling lines and machine shops. I'd worked as a cook, a dishwasher and a stock boy and I'd gutted houses ruined by fire or neglect. I'd loaded beer cases, scrap metal and boxes of lettuce and nails and feminine hygiene products. "Hell," I laugh, "if it comes in a box, chances are I've muscled it onto a truck."

She tells me about her first job as a fifteen-year-old camp counsellor. It was for normal kids, but one of the boys came along with a brother who obviously had something wrong with him. Maybe he was autistic, she says. His name was Richard, but everyone called him Ricky Butterfly because whenever a butterfly fluttered by, he'd chase after it, full tilt, on his skinny pinwheel legs.

Most of the kids laughed at him, even his brother in an embarrassed kind of way. The counsellors didn't like him because he needed constant supervision and the camp director wanted to send him home after Ricky Butterfly chased a cabbage moth out onto the road and almost got mashed by a logging truck.

But she wouldn't hear a word of it. She swore up and down that she would personally look after Ricky, and finally, after much debate, she convinced them all to let him stay. Even at fifteen she was a force that could not be denied.

"I made paper butterflies on the ends of Popsicle sticks to keep his attention," she tells me. "At first he was scared of the water, but I taught him to swim by himself. His mother cried when she saw him swimming in the relay race at the end of the summer." I can picture her running across fields, flapping her paper butterflies like a shaman, Ricky in happy pursuit. And I can see her in the water with Ricky, holding him afloat and imploring him to kick his legs and thrash his arms — magical incantations that, however briefly, coaxed that strange little boy out of his wilderness to dog-paddle side-by-side with his peers.

We sit there for a good long while without saying anything else. For the first time in my life I am comfortable with the silence, even grateful for it. Just the two of us, hidden from the rest of the world in the perfect oxbow bend of one of the millions of rivers I have never sat beside. I fall in love with that woman at that exact moment and I wish that we would never leave, pray the earth would creak to a halt and the sunbathers down river would pack up their empties and everyone would just let us be.

But the sun starts to slip below the treeline and I can feel her shiver small beside me. I wrap her shoulders in the one dry towel, but I can tell she is cold. "Maybe we should go," I say, hating myself for knowing those four words.

She looks at me with her black Basque eyes and I know that there is a message there, a key. But I have never been good in the wild; I lose my bearings outside my metropolitan grids. She can't be read, at least not by me. "Yes," she says, "let's go." And, simple as that, she drives me back to my friend's house.

It is only when I'm home in Montreal the next night that I think of all the things I should have said or done, think about the ways I've won women in the past. But in the back of my mind I know full well that my barroom strategies would never work there on the water where rivers carve their own destiny. I fall asleep imagining her beside me.

In the middle of the night, a violent clap of thunder startles me awake and sends my cats crabbing to the closet, bellies to the floor. The rain beats at the concrete down below and lightning illuminates my room in stuttering silver blasts. I sit upright, heart beating fast and hard, and catch my reflection in the mirror. For reasons I can't explain, I immediately know that the dark girl is back standing in the river, face turned upward, caressed and anointed by the same storm that, tonight, has revealed me alone and still afraid.

Anger on the Outskirts of Arcadia

She was fat. I mean really fat. With huge hanging tits and a monstrous, dimpled, bulbous arse. She was a little crazy too, liked being slapped around and treated like shit. Liked feeling my open hand come crashing down on her jiggling white crapper.

I swear to Christ, this one was middle-linebacker weight, 240 pounds. Easy. But she wasn't any taller than 5 foot 6. Just a sloppy-fat broad who got off from getting smacked around.

I had heard her ad on one of those telephone dating services where people leave a description of themselves and tell you what fleshy fetish puts the whirl in their whirly-bird. She was box 3401, in the "Submission and Domination" category. Unlike a lot of us desperados she wasn't full of shit when it came to describing herself. She came right out and told the world how she was a porker who enjoyed a bit of the kink, in her case, being tied up and flogged like some poor fucker in a medieval fun-factory.

I don't know why — up until then I had only listened to the ads — but I left a message right away. Cost me ten bucks on my next phone bill. I said something about wanting to paddle her white butt red. She called me back the next day and we arranged to meet at a doughnut shop.

Sweet fuck. She was bigger in real life than even her own blunt description of herself could have prepared me for. When she wedged herself into the seat in front of me I was disgusted. I just sat there, mute, waiting for her to order a dozen French twists and a tub of custard. Instead, she asked for a small coffee, no sugar, and smiled wryly at my thinly veiled surprise. But she didn't say anything, not a word, she just looked me up and down, sizing me up like I was a meat-loaf sandwich or something.

A couple of silent minutes later her coffee arrived. I was still staring, wanting desperately to get up and run screaming down the road, but I just sat there. Staring. She blew the steam off her coffee, took a sip and smiled menacingly. "So you like to beat women?" Her voice was bland, nondescript, invisible.

Oh shit, I felt sick knowing why I was there. Knowing I was going to do it. Nausea speed-bagged my belly and my fighting legs jellied. I was sweating like a whore in church.

She leaned forward, big fleshy white throat shimmering like lakewater under a sickly moon. "What's wrong," she asked, "don't like to talk? Good. Let's not talk anymore," and with that she was on her pinchy piggy feet, waddling out the door. And I, disgusted and wanting more than any-thing to bolt, followed closely behind.

Pimples, dimples, and unhealthy red blotches. The deepest, darkest, most menacing ass crack of all time. An ass crack for the ages. Without so much as a word, she walked straight into the room, number 214, peeled off her clothes, climbed onto the bed on all fours and buried her head in the pillows. She looked like a gigantic, hairless puppy wanting to play, butt in the air.

I had never been with a broad even half that huge. In fact, I took a certain pride in knowing that I had never been desperate or drunk enough to fuck a real fatty. But there I was gazing into the Grand Canyon of arses. A fucking monument to big shitters the world over.

So I slapped her. A little tentative at first — remember, I wasn't very experienced at this. A small shudder rattled down her spine and she notched those hungry mud flaps up a bit higher. I put a little elbow grease into the next one and smacked her with added oomph. She groaned and shook a bit, like my dad's old station wagon on a frosty winter day. I cranked her harder. And a little harder after that. *Pow. Crack. Bang.* Soon I was taking a running start from across the room, like some crazy fucking cricket pitcher. I windmilled my open palm down on her oversized poop cutters with absolute malice. I breathed heavy and my dick was hard. Now, I was sweating like a rapist.

Yeah, I know it sounds crazy, I know it *is* crazy, but she seemed to really get off on the violence. Every time I belted her it sent a jolt of feel-good way down inside her, like I had to hurt her deep just so she could feel something. Anything. Whatever, she really got off on all that hair pulling, blindfolding, ass-smacking, handcuffing stuff. The only thing was, she didn't have an orgasm. She never came. Every Wednesday night for seven months I had that crazy fat bitch roped and tied and moaning and twitching like a great tub of happy pink Jell-O, but she'd never come. I know why, of course: I never touched her pussy. Ever.

See, she had this tiny pussy hiding under all those grotesque layers of suet. A little girl's private parts; a shy baby thing nestled in delicate soft curls. I'd spend hours spanking her fat shit locker with all my might and crashing her big tits together like great gods of war. I'd ram fingers up her butt, my cock in her mouth and I'd come in her face, on her jugs and all over that never-ending ass crack. But I couldn't bring my dirty self to touch her pussy.

It almost made me shy, like it was an innocent witness to my nastiness and loathing. See, I spend all day, all week, all fucking year, fighting the anger, tying it up and strapping it down. But it struggles and twists and strains at the bonds. It's exhausting and terrifying, because when it does bust loose it bubbles over and spills out onto the street like gunpowder-tinged blood. A prison break.

It slashes and cuts and comes at me hard and fearless, a lunatic with a broken bottle. It overwhelms the workaday me, the guy-next-door me, the socialized me who talks politics and hockey and tells forgettable off-colour jokes to co-workers and bartenders and guys in the gym. It pistol-whips me into a corner and hands over the cage keys to the ugly brute beast I've kept locked away since I was a brooding bastard kid. I didn't mind beating that crazy fat chick. She seemed to like it, even need it in a way I'd never understand — but something about her pussy shamed me. Made me want to cover up and hide.

Now, maybe you last few Freudians want to hear how my earliest memory of my mom is of her naked in a bathtub, highball in hand, nipples like raspberries topping off cream-coloured breasts. And maybe the armchair psychiatrists would be better able to label me like an entomologist's dead butterfly, pin through the heart, if they knew that during two periods of my youth I tortured small animals. And maybe it would simplify things, rationalize them, if I told you that once a month my old man would march us four boys down to his workroom and belt-whip us whether we deserved it or not. And maybe I would garner the sympathy of sociologists and psychologists and all the world's other apologists if they knew that between the ages of eight and eleven, I had a hockey coach, the grandfatherly Mr. Granger, who would make me jerk him off like a circus monkey whenever he drove me home.

Yeah, maybe it would help you all sleep better at night knowing there is a reason why I carry this hatred in me, why a white, middle-class, well-educated boy went so bad. To paraphrase Marx: cause and effect is the opiate of the people. The weak people. You hope all my ills can be explained away in a broad, sweeping, comforting stroke, because if they can be so neatly categorized and compartmentalized, then maybe, just maybe, they can be cured. Cured before your daughter finds herself alone in Room 214 with me.

Unfortunately there is no easy way out of this one because none of those life-defining moments — not mummy's tits, not daddy's whippings, not the tortured animals, not the pedophilia — belong to me. My childhood was simple and perfectly uneventful, just an endless loop of summer camps and snowball fights and cellophane-wrapped quarters buried like treasure in birthday cakes.

But still I seethe for no apparent reason, at least none that I can finger. The anger is just there in my cells, in my genes, woven like barbed-wire strands in my DNA. And I'm not the only one; I recognize the same blood-sport glint in the eyes of white middle classers everywhere. Middle-management types riding the metro and grimacing on the stairmaster. Bus drivers and teachers. Me and the laughing guy on my elbow at the bar. Buckle up people, this privileged class kicks ass — or at least beats it to within an inch of its life.

So, luckily for your plaid-skirted daughter, that fat chick's giant arse was the conductor of all my rage. Like a fleshy lightning rod, it drew from me all my electric hatred and every imperfection that made me ball up my fists under my desk while my boss chewed me out. I began seeing the faces of people who pissed me off in each purple bruise and pinkish blotch. *There!* Mr. Jameson — the first cocksucking coach who ever ridiculed me and made the team do push-ups whenever I dropped a fly ball. *Crack!* Kelly — my ex-girlfriend who dumped me for a dyke with hockey hair. *Smack!* My polack landlord. *Slap!* The rude bitch cashier at the corner store. The piss-smelling bum who sleeps in my stairwell. That smug, burly cop. My arsehole brother. Dogs who shit on the sidewalk. All fucking Jehovah's Witnesses. *Crash! Wham! Pow! Smash! Bang!*

"Oh my!" she'd moan from the pillow.

By the end of each session her ass glowed hard like steamed lobster. *Red, red, red* — an angry, violent, and dangerous red sucked from my eyes and heart, yanked from my guts like a fetus gone horribly wrong. Week after week she took, begged for, the blood-red bile that flash-flooded through my veins and filled my stomach with razored edges.

Her ass would accept the very worst of me, the stuff that keeps me awake at night shaking and crying, and it burned with it; a living ember fueled entirely by my venom. In some weird, Daliesque way that ass became an entity unto itself. Alive with my hate, it hung above us both, above us all: the North Star to small angry mariners and sociopaths and pissed off wise men everywhere. But when next week lurched around, I'd bust through door 214 to be greeted by that white, terribly white, ass. By then it had processed all my torments and beatings and absorbed them like a huge flesh sponge. Her cream-coloured butt just hung there, *tabula rasa,* waiting patiently for me to carve another week's worth of rage upon it.

When it was all over, I'd collapse on her belly or between her fat thighs, panting like a poisoned dog. Her skin was hot and wet and with every breath her horrifying body would ripple with tiny rhythmic waves, a living waterbed. I'd be so exhausted from all that ass-slapping and nipple-twisting and hair-pulling that I couldn't move. Didn't want to. Lying there, I floated in that flesh ocean, drifting away into the liquid whiteness. Away. My sweat, my heartbeat, my strength, my violence — all enveloped by her huge, receptive frame. Week after week I'd give in to her vastness.

I'd sprawl out with my head on one of her fat folds, staring right at her tiny pussy. It was an island, an undiscovered Greek enclave. I was bobbing in an ocean of pimples and ugliness, numb and exhausted but always aware, however instinctively, that the sea swells were carrying me toward paradise, my Arcadia. Floating. Drifting. Closer and closer and closer still. Cognition stopped, warm sensations returned. I thought I would sleep, but I know I didn't. She breathed for me and each breath whispered "peace."

Every night ended the same way. After a while, maybe hours, she'd gently roll me off of her, cover me with a sheet, get dressed and leave. I remember all this but I can't say I ever saw it or heard it. I was always still adrift, so close to serenity.

But when she'd leave, the metallic click of the door would echo low thunder across the open water of my dreamscape, and Arcadia was nowhere to be seen on the distant, foreboding horizon. Suddenly, I was mindful that I was between realities, the dreamer who sadly understands he's only dreaming.

With this awareness came the disintegration of hopeful reverie and the resurrection of bastard thought. One by one, the sounds and smells and textures of this ugly life, my motel existence, would barge into the liquid white world of drifting. Car horns, cheap scratchy sheets, the practised moans of the whore next door, sirens, the stink of spilled beer, sweat and sex. My heartbeat. And then there I was, lying on my side staring at myself in the mirror on the wall with vacant eyes. For the first few merciful minutes I'd feel nothing, nothing at all. But the air-conditioned cold would snake up my skin, slide in my ass and ears and nose and chill me through. Chill me like death. Chill me like curse. Chill me like my every day. And in my gut I would feel the bitter new bud of hatred send out its first tentative shoot.

In a Hotel Room Overlooking the Trevi Fountain

We are young, making love that afternoon, again that night and another time the next morning. Once we do it at the window, both of us gazing at the magnificent fountain below. The motionless statues mock our mortal struggles, as we move in fruitless search of love's immortality. Your thick breath off my neck, your saliva running through my mouth like sweet eels; both will cool one day and then cease altogether. But Trevi's Neptune rises from the perfect man-made waves astride a chariot drawn by two muscular horses, forever caught between wind and water.

Twice we do it on the overstuffed bed, laughing from the verdant valley floor of our downy mattress. Rome's humid air slides across our salty hips and shoulders, a lover's tongue on lovers' skin. Four stories up from the fountain, our gasps fly skyward on the back of water's winged splash, like ghostly ash resurrecting from fire. Heard by no one, except ledge-bound pigeons, gargoyles and God.

Earlier that day, we had eaten grapefruits on the Spanish Steps. The fruit was fat, but mealy and dry. It was the only time Rome disappointed me.

For me, grapefruits are an erotic fruit. Back in our first apartment so many years ago, we would lie in bed on Sunday mornings and snuff our hunger pangs with them. At first, you had to order me to stay there beside you. I viewed bed as a diabolical trap designed to keep me from getting on with my day. There were muscles to train, stories to write, friends to carouse with and beer to guzzle.

But you decreed that Sundays were to share in bed and I've always had a hard time saying no to you. We'd spend all day drifting in and out of sleep, always reaching over to touch the body, the face, the hair; like warm-blooded vines stretching for the sun. You taught me that even asleep these are shared moments, that the body has memory and con-sciousness. Every time we pressed together, incidentally or otherwise, our sleeping midnight selves were as soothed and invigorated as with a full embrace at high noon. Today, no matter how well I've slept, I wake up alone on Sundays and my body aches with remembrance of you and our time.

Parched and hungry, I'd sneak out of bed and cart back an armload of grapefruits. I've always been greedy. I'd wolf them down, dripping their juices onto my naked lap, and curl myself around the supple invitation of your body. My juicy hands would cup your breasts and trace fingertips over the crescent moon scar where doctors removed the lump. I'd wind myself around your thighs and neck and pubic bone, and you'd stir and call me a pervert. When I buried my lips in the chancel of your collarbone, your whole body smelled strongly of sweat and sex and sweet grapefruit. The tingle of love's fruit bit my lips. Now I can't eat grapefruit without getting nostalgic and a hard-on.

But there on the Spanish Steps, what little juice lurked in our grapefruits squirted out their ass ends when we pierced our thumbs into their hearts and ripped them apart. The clear sweetness leaked down your fingers, and when you scratched your cheek it was left smudged with Rome's centuries old dirt. Caesar's dirt. Nero's dirt. Now, your dirt.

"Enough," you laughed, after I'd inspired you to open-mouthed yawns with stories of Shelley and Keats hanging out in Rome's English Ghetto, stories I had gleaned from books back in the sunless bowels of Montreal libraries. "Let's check out Trevi Fountain," you said and pulled me from my squat on the rounded steps, shaking the dust off your ass with your trademark shimmy. On the landing midway up the stairs, two wiry cops watched your lovely butt dance in the summer dress. They had their hats pulled down characteristically low so I couldn't see their eyes, but their smiles spoke of absolute admiration. Italians have a good eye for asses. *Bella culo.*

Following our map, we turned up a side street so small I thought we were lost. I'd read about the fountain's size and magnificence and was sure its grandeur could only be contained in an expansive piazza. "Listen," you grinned, and I listened. Running water. Taking a small bend in the alleyway we came upon it, the Trevi Fountain.

A million events happen during the course of a person's lifetime, but most are quickly forgotten. Some stick out for obvious reasons; your first kiss; the birth of your children; a doctor floating the word *cancer* into the air.

But others, like my first view of Trevi, put a hook in you forever for reasons you can't explain. Standing behind you, I wrap you up in my arms and press open palms on your flat stomach. I'm not one for babies, but at that exact moment I wish I could feel one kick. I don't know why, maybe I just wish that, right then and there, we shared something that would outlast us. Guiding my hand up to your mouth, you grace its callused palm with a kiss. You say nothing but your lips are eloquent with love.

Running low on money, but flying high on happiness, we do what comes naturally for us — we say "fuck tomorrow" and rent a $400 hotel room overlooking the fountain. One night, just like the commercials. We'll go hungry for the rest of our time in Rome, hungry until we make it back to your uncle's place in Florence and gorge ourselves on razor-thin slices of prosciutto. So be it. In Rome we will fatten our souls instead.

Bursting into our room, we throw open the wooden shutters that I thought only existed in Hollywood's Italy. I'm mesmerized by the fountain, especially by the marble horses hauling Neptune's chariot. Both are being lead by the mane by muscular Tritons blowing conch shells, both churning eternally from the ocean's foam. Heroism forever shared by earth, sea and sky. One horse rears angrily at being so bridled to servitude, the other charges stoically straight ahead. One so agitated, one so placid — could there be a more perfect representation of you and I?

You are the agitated one, the half-wild woman born in a tiny mountain village three hours east of Rome. So small it isn't even on the map. When you were eight, your family moved to Montreal where you became well-versed in cosmopolitan ways. You started off as a cosmetician in a pharmacy who disco-danced at the roller rink in fuzzy skates, and you changed for no one, dazzling your way up corporate ladders without kissing a single ass. Even as a successful business-woman years later, you'd bring clients out to the city's last remaining roller rink for a night of beer, Bee Gees and belly laughs.

But you are still half wild. Three days ago, I had to pull you from the Sistine Chapel after you went for the throat of a thick-thighed German who, along with some 50 others, was ignoring the recorded messages to refrain from using flash cameras. Thousands of tourists pour through the chapel every day, each small explosion of their cameras fading by infinitesimal degrees the sublime scene looming above them. The figurehead guards say nothing, do nothing.

Only you cared that Michelangelo's art should last beyond the moment caught so poorly on film. It was as if you alone could see the bare ceiling swimming like a patient shark beneath the masterpiece. You thrust your hand in front of the cameras of a gaggle of Japanese and stared down a reed-thin American who swaggered in like a sheriff dangling a holster full of strobes and flashes. You looked at me with sad eyes, eyes that understood that nothing, not even great art, lasts forever.

We stand naked at the window and take pictures of Trevi all afternoon. They will end up being horrible pictures, perfectly focused and well lit, but criminally small. Too small. Like squeezing the Rockies onto a postcard. The Bible on the head of a pin. My love for you into words on paper.

We fling a coin into the fountain from our window because legend says that lovers who do so will one day return. Brown, shirtless boys — running xylophones of ribs and white teeth — link arms and lean into the water to abscond with handfuls of sun-flashed silver before the self-important fountain guard scatters them with his whistle. You laugh large at the scene playing out below, but I secretly pray that our solitary coin remained long enough for the magic to set.

Your thin arm snakes itself around my waist and you pull me into bed. We've always made love well, but this day is even better. Our bodies glide like water dancing over marble, and our hands are those of sculptors, fashioning beauty and greatness that, though not lasting, is sublime like mountains. Afterward, I unwind myself from your sleeping arms and take my perch by the window to watch the sun set.

You wake up twice and call my name. Once, after they had shut off the fountain's spotlights, you join me at the sill. Like the statues below, we are painted silver by the fat, harvest moon. We make love again, you sitting on my lap gracing my neck with whispered stories of your childhood.

You were born atop your family's kitchen table, the town priest sliding you out from between your mother's heavy, splayed legs as she cried for God's benevolence. Because it was November 1st, All Saints' Day, your wonderfully operatic mother wanted to call you Santa, Italian for saint. But the priest, the always-smiling Father Moletti, laughed that it was too big a responsibility to place on such a small creature. Instead, he convinced your parents to call you Caramanna, his mother's name. "My brothers and I were holy terrors," he winked. "Trust me, mama was a saint in her own right."

A week after Trevi, we would drive up the narrow, winding road leading to your village, honking at curves to warn others coming the other way to squeeze over and let us through. Halfway up, we stopped at a clearing and you pointed to a fast-running creek where you and the children swam and caught water spiders. Mountains roll out to the horizon, one folding into the other like a giant rumpled quilt.

It was easy to imagine Caramanna, the child, in this setting — bold, happy, independent. Running loose along the trails where ill-tempered mountain boars still trundled, afraid of nothing, exploring everything. Your voice — already too earthy for a little girl of six or seven — must have ricocheted down the road to the valley below, warning everyone to make room.

We stayed in your village for ten days and all the remaining inhabitants, numbering no more than 40, told me the same story. As a child you were all movement and mischief, hands on your hips staring everyone straight in the eye. Adults would shoo you away with whimsical grins, chiding that little girls should not understand so much as to be able to make eyes like that at their elders. Elbows, knees and that long, hooked nose —a little girl wrapped in a boy's hard angles and a man's hearty laugh.

Father Moletti, still alive and happily absolving sins, smiled wide at our impetuous request to be married on the spot, obviously tickled to see that your headlong rush hadn't been slowed down by adulthood. That morning, we had woken up in your birth-house to watch wisps of dawn's fog snake up the mountainside, carrying on their backs the ethereal truths of tradition and symbolism. Until that moment, we had both been avowedly anti-marriage. But we knew that this was too perfect — to be married in the church where you had been baptized, by the same man who had drawn you gently into this world.

The old priest squeezed our shoulders. His hands were warm and weighty, as adept at yanking stubborn roots from his garden as they were at sliding the body of Christ into waiting mouths. "This isn't Las Vegas," he grinned. "No quickie marriages here. Post it for a year and we'll talk." We agreed to do so, but once outside the church we laughed hard at our recklessness and our close escape.

Our fountain coin must have been snatched away too quickly, because we would never make it back to your village, never make it back to Italy. We would never marry. Yes, we may have escaped, but today I realize that the price for that freedom was heavy.

Back in Montreal, you'd tell friends that I spent the whole night at Trevi sitting at the window watching the fountain. What you didn't know is that I spent as much time watching you sleep. Although we had been living together for ten years, it was as if only then — that very night — I had stumbled onto your beauty. Your face, the fountain, both are revealed to me during the night. We think that, once dark, night is all the same. But it isn't. Every hour has its subtle difference, as does each sunlit moment during the day.

At 1 a.m., you are lovely like baby pictures and the fountain is still busy, with couples spacing themselves in the low, concrete stands so that their intimate duets leave no trace, swallowed by the water's rush. An hour later, your face is strong, the tough-talking neighbourhood girl who I had first fallen in love with through the pharmacy's rounded anti-shoplifting mirrors. Neptune is wrapped in a black cloak of shadow as an ominous cloud blocks out the moon.

At 3 a.m., a group of gossiping city workers hose down the area from a bulky water truck. A solitary couple scatters, jumping from their fountain-side altar and running down the cobblestone, arms tied around each other like ribbons. The clickety-clack of high heels ricochets to the rooftops. I look at you and see a face full of lessons waiting yet for me to learn.

At dawn, I kiss your lips with the promise that I'll soon return. I run from our hotel to the Spanish Steps, hopping over sleeping Scandinavian teenagers on my way to the top. Huffing, I reach the summit just as the sun glints off the burnished dome of San Pietro and illuminates the scaffolding propping up the crumbling Colosseo. Sunrise over Rome, each day born anew. I wish you were with me but I know how much sleep an agitated horse like you needs.

I snap more useless photos, ever the desperate tourist trying to preserve my Kodak moments. When I run out of film, I head back. It's not yet six o'clock and already people are gathering. What will they leave here with, after such a brief audience with Trevi? I smile and look up at our window. These people will never really know the fountain.

Upstairs, I want to kiss you awake and kiss you back to sleep again. Instead, I tiptoe back to the window. This time Trevi makes me sad. In Rome's virgin light I can see thin cracks spider-webbing like surgery across Neptune's forehead. The night was so short and our checkout time looms so large. Later, we'll enjoy our complimentary continental breakfast (toast and more grapefruit) from the terrace on the roof, but soon after that we'll be gone.

I didn't know it then, but even as you lay there coiled in Trevi's magic, cancer was once again spreading its thin, fibrous fingers through you. A malignant fist unclenching in your breast and reaching deep to take deadly hold of your liver, blood and brain. It would take years, mind you, but the disease would win, its victory trail marked by milestones of medical procedures that you endured. Chemo, radiation, stem-cell transplants, hourly cocktails of coloured pills, a double mastectomy — you lost your hair, your breasts and eventually your laugh.

At the end, you died in my embrace, skeletal, gaunt and sallow, but still my *bella Caramanna*. You were barely heavier than a baby, I thought at the time. Barely heavier than breath. Holding you in my arms, I filled your ear with happy stories of your childhood and I rocked you softly from our life together into solitary death.

Turning to the bed I catch your face perfectly asleep and peaceful. Finally, the placid horse like me. The city is not yet sweating and a cool morning breeze washes over your brow and lips, beautiful and unmarked by time or pain. I want to hold on to this moment and never let go, clutching it to my chest until death alone loosens my grasp.

I pray for us to be turned to statues, pray that our time together could last the centuries, and that love was infinite just because I wrote it so. But Rome blows its secret whispers in your ear and you stir. Your eyes flutter open and you smile your wild, wondrous love at me. How can I refuse this gift, fashioned by saints on their day and delivered to us all by a smiling man of God? I join you in your cocoon of comforters and we celebrate another day of our life together, a day unlike all the others that came before and all those that we've yet to share. But even as we selflessly pass our breath from one to another in a kiss, the new sun above slips one second closer to setting. One day, even Trevi will crumble.

Acknowledgements

Some of these Stories have appeared in *Pagitica*, *Exile: The Literary Quarterly*, and *SubTerrain*. "Honey-Tongued Hooker" won the CBC-QWF Short Story competition in 2000, and was broadcast on CBC Montreal's *Arts Talk*